IN PURSUIT OF KINGDOMS

ALSO BY THE AUTHOR

The Legend Begins

In Pursuit of Kingdoms

The Rule of Benedict

Augustine of Canterbury

IN PURSUIT OF KINGDOMS

R.G.J. MACKINTOSH

AWAKENED PUBLISHING
awakenedpublishing.com ©2021
Rob Mackintosh
All Rights Reserved.

To my wife Gillian,
In the making of this book;
- And to all my Companions,
Sharing the Journey.

PREFACE

AD 597 in the Kingdom of Cantia:

It's not every day that ghosts of the long-dead return without warning, to the grieving lives they once left behind.

This was such a day.

For Alric and his closest companions, homecoming in C7th Saxon Kingdom of Cantia is both the most joyous yet also the hardest experience of all, made even more difficult by an unexpected arrival from Rome.

Over the next five decades, fulfilling the Pope's mission has no shortage of opposition: alliances, romance, warring kingdoms, dynastic rivalries, life and death challenges, successions, power-struggles – and most of all, lasting friendships.

Alric and his companions face many challenges against the new religion they bring: soothsayers, powerful Saxon Earls, and not least, an encounter with the Bishops of the British Kingdoms.

Now Alric arrives at a crossroads, awaiting the last opportunity for his final Quest.

CHAPTERS

1.	Homecoming
2.	Ratteburg Fort
3.	King Ethelbert
4.	Coningsburh
5.	Oestre
6.	Something of Value
7.	Ethelbert's Baptism
8.	The First-fruits
9.	Cathedral
10.	Return to Rome
11.	Gregorian Letters
12.	The Wedding
13.	New faces from Rome
14.	Turn of the Tide
15.	The Passing
16.	Victorinus
17.	Long Live The King
18.	Traitors' Gate
19.	Laurentius
20.	Stirrings in the North
21.	A Generation Rising
22.	A Birthday Celebration
23.	Return to Lyminge
24.	The Last Quest

I

HOMECOMING, SANDWIC HAVEN,

April, AD 597

IT'S NOT EVERY day that ghosts of the long dead return without warning to the grieving lives they once left behind.

This was such a day.

With my eyes wet with tears and a lump in my throat, I stared at the grey foaming sea, the prow of the ship rising and falling on an incoming tide. Beyond the stern, the Kingdom of the Franks dropped away and the shores of the Kingdom of Cantia drew ever closer. Tola, my sister, stood beside me in the prow, her midnight-black hair blowing loose in the wind and her lips trembling as the ship swept towards the landing place of Sandwic Haven. Squeezing Tola's hand, I strained to glimpse the quay.

Our immediate destination was Sandwic Haven, a large natural harbour scoured by the ebb and flow of the tides. For Tola and me, the Haven was the most significant landmark in the world, with tall oaks and weeping willows fringing the shoreline. From within a wooden stockade at the close of day, smoke from dozens of fires curled into the evening sky.

Tola and I glanced briefly at each other; was this finally happening? I looked up at the gulls swooping and screeching high above the mast, and taking a deep breath I shouted into the wind the words that I hardly dared to believe.

"We are coming home!"

Cadmon my closest friend stood beside us, feet apart, rolling with the pitch of the ship. Behind us, standing with one hand on the mast, Bishop Augustinus absorbed every detail of an unfolding landscape he had never seen before. In the stern, Felix the skipper steered from a raised wooden platform, a scowl darkening his face. I glared at him and I said under my breath, "You took us from our home by stealth, against our will and without mercy. Now seven long years have passed, Felix, but justice waits for you no longer!"

*

I hugged farewell to Cadmon and Augustinus, dropped onto the landing, and reached up to take Tola and her few possessions. Waving farewell as the ship slipped away towards Cadmon's home at Ratteburg, we stood together trembling, and feeling completely alone. A high wooden enclosure encircling the Haven stood some yards back from the water's edge. My fishing traps were there as I had left them. I looked down the length of the quay. The gateway, through which we had once been dragged onto Felix's ship, stood half-open.

"Hello," I called out to a young lad of thirteen or so years, working with his nets on the far side. He watched our arrival for a few moments and then hauled himself out of the water. His hair was dark, like Pa's, his build stockier than mine, and his face wore a puzzled frown.

"Godric?" I queried, coming closer. The youngster's expression did not change. Godric had not recognised me; and in truth, I found it difficult to recognise him. He nodded at the sound of his name, switching his stare from me to Tola, and back again. He looked confused.

"Godric! I'm your brother—Alric. And this is our sister, Tola."

As he came closer, I noticed Godric's features were more like Mama's.

"Godric, our father's name is Galen, and our mother is Erlina, and our younger sister is Greta. Today we have returned after a long, long journey. Is everyone well?"

Godric had remained totally silent since our arrival.

"Come!" Tola said gently, stepping forward and kissing Godric on the cheek.

"Take us to Mama and Pa!"

Godric turned abruptly on his heel, and we marched swiftly behind him into the compound. As we entered, I ran my hand over the wooden gate and felt the wet grass underfoot. The thatched roofs of the hovels almost touched the ground. The first hovel—our home with Ma and Pa—was freshly thatched, and a few new sheds stood further up the slope towards the rear of the stockade, where a wooden fence held back a dense forest of oak and elm.

Men, women and children went back and forth about their business. Not much seemed to have changed in seven years. I became aware of the sounds of wood chopping, hens clucking and scratching around in the yard, pigs grunting and a woodpecker high in a tree hammering away, close by the water.

Already, Rome seemed a distant memory.

Godric glanced sideways at me a couple of times, and I prodded, "Don't you remember the last time we were together? Two of our dark hairy pigs with pointy ears escaped because the back gate was open, and you came back from the dark and scary woods to tell Pa, and I was standing next to him, at the smoking shed."

Godric glanced at me again and lengthened his stride so that he was a little ahead of us, walking faster now, then running, running and calling out.

"Pa! Mama! Alric and Tola are back! They're here! They've come home!"

It was the word "home" that finally cracked my flimsy mask of self-composure. With my throat constricted tears flowed, and Godric was still running, still shouting.

"They're here, Mama! They're back!"

Ahead of us, Pa left off chopping logs for the fire and wiped his hands on a cloth as he stared down the path towards us. Closer by, with a bucket in her hand, Ma looked out of the doorway of our family hovel—the hovel that no longer needed the extension Pa had planned for his growing family, because their two oldest children had vanished in the morning mist on a slave ship. Now, two youngsters who were last seen here at the ages of eight and ten years, looked like ghostly apparitions.

"Mama!" Tola rushed forward as fast as her white habit would allow, throwing back her head-covering so that her long, dark hair flowed onto her shoulders, running like the whirlwind into Mama's open arms.

Godric ran ahead of me and reached Pa first. He had grown nearly as tall as Galen himself. Screams and cries were rising from Erlina and Tola at the hovel behind us as I came to a standstill outside the smoking shed.

Pa looked at me. He had hardly changed.

We stared at each other.

Swallowing hard, all I could say as my voice broke was, "Pa. It's me. Alric."

Incredulous, my father Galen swore an oath, dropped his heavy axe and we reached out for one another in a crushing hug, standing back then another hug as years of hell and loss and tears struck with all the force of a raging storm.

Helga, my aunt, emerged from her hovel, while Greta—my sister, 'little Greta' no more—left off weaving and ran down to join Erlina and Tola, hugging, and weeping in disbelief. In a few minutes the entire village knew of our arrival and flooded out to share this incredible, unexpected reunion unfolding before their eyes.

*

Later, we sat outside the mead hall on the grassy logs, telling our stories, answering questions and asking after the welfare of everyone that we once knew at the Haven, half a lifetime ago. We laughed, we cried, we talked, we remembered and we started all over again. Night came, a huge fire was lit, food was cooked and drink was served. We celebrated until the late moon rose and the young ones needed their beds. Then the elderly too, and soon workingmen and women needing their strength for the morrow, also drifted away.

At last, our reunited family fell into a deep sleep in our small, clean, beautiful hovel, a place like no place on earth. All except Mama, who did not want to close her eyes, not even for a moment, afraid that in the coming of dawn we would disappear again like wraiths, and all that she had witnessed was merely another sickening, disappointing dream.

Mama finally drifted into sleep until, at first light, a hand gently shook her shoulder and lips softly kissed her cheek. When she opened her eyes, Tola was kneeling beside her. The two women clung to each other, and their weeping began once again.

*

After breakfast Pa, Godric and I set off in our boat to cut reeds for the roof of the new shed. Pa began cutting while Godric threw out his line, hauling in large numbers of fish. Pa handed me bunches of reeds and I tied the top and bottom with twine before throwing them into the boat. After only a few minutes it was clear to me that Godric was a far better fisherman than me.

Later, back at the Haven, Pa asked, "Tell me about this monastery you've been staying at." I had noticed that our old shrine to Neorth the sea-god still remained, and from my look, Pa understood I no longer had any confidence in the old gods, but I did not want to erect a barrier with our family. Bishop Augustinus had cautioned us on our journey home, "You must make time to listen, Alric, and simply be with your family and others you have known. Without their trust, whatever we say will never make any difference in their lives."

I knew then it would be no easy matter to tell my family about

Christ replacing Wodin and all the other gods. Why had I imagined otherwise? My great joy on returning to the Haven was now evenly matched by a great emptiness. How was I going to explain everything we had seen and done, and what we had learned? And what were my own hopes for the future now?

Even so, and because he asked, I told Pa about my feelings, how neither Wodin nor Neorth, the god of the waters, came to our aid in our desperate hour of need.

"Why do we make offerings to them, Pa? Aren't they supposed to help *us*? In Rome, it was the monks who came to our rescue. They took good care of Cadmon and me. They educated us, and we had a plenty of people to give us support. That's how Cadmon was able to join the Cavalry. And there were miracles too."

I told of all that had happened, both in Rome and more recently on our journey through the Kingdoms of Francia. As we talked together, Pa surprised me, recalling that in his youth his family had worshipped the Christian God, but he had lost touch with both his family and his faith since marrying Erlina.

But also, I sensed resentment from Godric. He had been their only son for half of his life, and adjusting to a new order would be hard for him. He had said disturbingly little the whole of our time together at the Haven. Unlike everyone else heaping endless questions on me, Godric had pointedly asked only one question as we settled down for our second night.

"When are you leaving?"

*

Overnight the weather had worsened, and in the morning the wind grew stronger. Nevertheless, it was time for Tola and me to rejoin Bishop Augustinus at Ratteburg for the next stage of our mission. We kissed Mama farewell and I hugged Pa, promising I'd bring Tola back soon.

Our farewell was an anticlimax. Pa said he was glad I had found work with the monks, somehow missing the point, but that wasn't his fault. I was glad Tola returned with me, not wanting to lose her too soon after all the months we had endured together through Francia. Of all my family, Tola was inevitably the one who truly understood me.

As our boat crossed the choppy waters to the ancient fort at Ratteburg, my thoughts returned to Paulina, my beloved Paulina, working at the convent of San Quattro Coronati in Rome. My heartache troubled me still. I shook my head to clear my thoughts and calm my feelings. I said to Tola, "So much longing went into our homecoming after these lost years, that I gave no thought to what would happen the day after."

Tola understood. Returning home was neither the fulfilment of our lives nor the end of our longing for something more. But what was my calling, my quest, now?

As our boat approached the quay at Ratteburg, Tola broke her silence.

"I didn't find it easy saying goodbye to Mama and Pa, Alric. I know it'll only be a couple of days. But then what? I don't think either of us wants to return to fishing or weaving."

I nodded. "Everyone at the Haven seems to be coping well enough without us, Tola. Maybe that's a good sign," I said with a shrug and a touch of disappointment.

I felt despondent. In material goods, I possessed almost nothing—a monk's habit on my back, a stylus and wax tablet in my pocket, and a gold coin around my neck. Then I remembered conversations with Brother Petrus, my Latin Tutor, about his wish for me to pursue a path of teaching and scribing, ultimately perhaps following in his footsteps as tutor, so that the world would be a better place. His words of wisdom echoed in my mind.

"Everything you need is already within you, Alric. Trust yourself."

11
RATTEBURG FORT

April, AD 597

RATTEBURG FORT SQUATS on a low hill, the ancient walls of the fort dark and forbidding. Twice every day this small tidal island is surrounded by marsh, almost cutting us off from the mainland; but even at high tide a rider on horseback can cross the ancient Roman bridge to higher ground and reach the King's Royal Hall at Coningsburh—or ride to Earl Sighart's Eastringe estate that lies to the south.

As we landed, Cadmon and his father Sighart hurried down to greet us on the quay. We disembarked, Cadmon hugging Tola and me, glad to be with us again. Sighart sang our praises because we had helped bring his son home. Our joyful reunion was repeated as Cadmon's mother Odelinda came out to greet us.

She held my sister's face in her hands.

"My dearest Tola, how beautiful you have grown! And nearly as tall as me! Tell me, what did your family say when you came home after all this time? Come up to the Hall. Come, you must tell me everything!"

Sighart followed the two women towards the Mead Hall, laughing at their excitement. He turned and said, almost as an afterthought, "By the way, Cadmon, your brother is coming over from Eastringe this evening. You two can catch up with each other. He will be surprised to see you!"

"I'm sure he will," Cadmon smiled grimly as the Earl continued to the Hall, while

I seized the opportunity to talk privately with Cadmon.

"What's going on here?" I asked. "I see Felix's ship, but none of his crew. What's happening?"

Cadmon gestured towards an outbuilding near the Mead Hall.

"Felix and his crew are chained up in that shed, under guard, while my Father decides what should be done with them. He has asked for another magistrate to join him tomorrow to examine them, so they can decide what punishment should be meted out."

"And your father—does he know anything about your brother Derian's part in all this?"

"Not a word. My father expects the two of us will be happily reunited! As yet he doesn't know of Felix's claim that it was Derian who paid for my abduction. I need his witness—but Felix can never be trusted!"

*

Bishop Augustinus greeted us as we entered the Hall.

"I have received word from the King!" Augustinus announced to all forty of our companions as we gathered together. "King Ethelbert wants us to remain here at Ratteburg, and he will come to us. There are many arrangements he needs to make first, so the exact timing is uncertain. But it's a good sign that he has agreed to give us a hearing!"

Earl Sighart elaborated. "The King will want to summon some of his chief men from other parts of the Kingdom to join with him here. If our meeting with Ethelbert finishes with us accompanying the King to Coningsburh, that would be a very good sign. But for now, here's our Bishop's plan of action."

In the Mead Hall a few candles were lit and a cask of beer placed on the table. Augustinus outlined a plan for conducting the meeting with the King, using several tumblers to show where various groups of our mission would stand. Again and again, we rehearsed the choreography of our upcoming meeting with Ethelbert.

Afterwards, as we sat at the tables, Sighart poured beer into the tumblers and said,

"Queen Bertha's influence with the King will be very important if your mission is to receive a favourable reception. She has wanted a mission such as this for years—and now, here you are!"

He reached out across the table to Cadmon and me, clasping our hands as he shook his head, eyes brimming. Gathering his composure he said, "For me, *this* is a miracle! Whatever happens when the King comes, I want you to know how grateful Odelinda and I are for what you have done, bringing all three of these young people home to us!"

Sighart released his iron grip and sat back again, calming himself with a deep breath, and returned to the matter of the King's arrival.

"Bishop, you and your companions will need to wait here in the Hall until after the King has landed. Then he will decide where he wants to sit to receive you."

Prior Laurentius, our Bishop's second in command, snorted. "Does he think he's the Emperor?"

Augustinus glared. Cadmon did not bother to translate. Sighart was puzzled, but Augustinus urged him to continue.

"The King will want to avoid meeting with you indoors, so you won't be able to use magic to trick him! When he is settled, he will summon you to meet him out in the open air. He will come with his Royal Guard, together with Queen Bertha, and their two sons, Eadbald and Ethelwald." Sighart paused a moment then added, "The younger son, Ethelwald, has ... shall we say, problems with his legs. He has been that way since his birth."

"That must be a great trial for the family," Augustinus agreed, and we sat in silence for a few moments.

Brother Petrus said, "Have you decided who will translate for you, Bishop?"

I had assumed that Cadmon would translate. Augustinus turned to address him.

"Cadmon, you have been our truly outstanding protector ever since we left Rome. You have fulfilled everything we asked of you, and much, much more. But I ask you to continue with us until we finish our audience with the King, and he has made up his mind as to our fate. At that point, your commission in this mission is discharged, so you can return to your father's estate, or to your Cavalry Unit in Rome, or whatever else you choose to do. Be ready, in full uniform, until our meeting with the King is done."

Bishop Augustinus then turned to me.

"And you, Alric, *you* will be the translator for our meeting with King Ethelbert!"

*

That evening we returned to the Mead Hall, greeted by a large, carefully tended log fire sunk into the floor at the centre of the Hall. Tables ran along three sides, illuminated by clusters of flickering tallow candles. Our forty companions added to the number of farmers, labourers, builders and warriors also seated at tables. Jugs of beer flowed freely and the feasting began. The Hall grew noisier, the mood becoming more raucous with laughter and challenges, while singing toasts as we celebrated Cadmon's return.

I became aware that Derian had entered the Hall. Rooted to the spot, he stared in disbelief at the brother he had never expected, nor ever wanted, to see again. In appearance, the two barely passed as siblings. The older brother was heavy-set, hair straggly, his small mouth pouting in a permanent look of displeasure. He stared at Cadmon, whose face was expressionless as his eyes bored into Derian's.

Sighart waved his older son to come over.

"Come, Derian! Come and greet your long-lost brother!"

The ancient story of the Prodigal Son flashed into mind.

"Come!" The Earl beckoned. "Let's make a place for you at the table."

A platter of wild boar was placed in front of him. Derian sat down opposite Sighart, making no eye contact with his brother.

"Let me tell you my story," Cadmon began. "Seven years ago I was seized at the Haven, along with Alric and Tola." Cadmon gestured towards Tola, sitting alongside Odelinda, and Derian's eyes widened as his gaze fell upon her.

"After a long, freezing journey of several months in the dark days of winter, we finally came to Rome to be sold as slaves. A community of holy men showed pity on us there; they bought our freedom and gave us shelter. And now, we have returned home with two score men, led by Augustinus our Bishop, to meet with the King. Oh, you might be interested to know that the name of the skipper who brought us home today is Felix. A strange twist of fate don't you think, as it was Felix who took us from the Haven? He and his crew are chained in one of the outbuildings, awaiting justice in the morning. I am sure they will have much to tell us! We want to hear from Felix who it was that paid him for dragging us into slavery!"

In the flickering yellow glow from candles in the Hall, Derian's face turned a sickly pallor. He rose abruptly.

"I've had a long journey. Excuse me." Cadmon waited a few moments before he also made his way to the door, slipping into the night after Derian.

Sighart, deep in conversation with Augustinus, barely registered their departure. Augustinus turned to me. "Alric, we must write some of this down. Could you bring a writing tablet and a sheet of parchment from the cart, and take some notes?" I arose at once and slipped out on my errand.

There was a chill wind and dark clouds partially obscured the moon, casting a spell over the black waters of the Wantsum Channel. I made my way to our circle of carts, packed with the tools and equipment we brought from Rome, pulled back one of the thick covers, and fished around in the dark. A little distance away I noticed someone dismissing the night guard. That could only have been Derian. I felt sick to the pit of my stomach, and I glanced back towards the Mead Hall. Another figure, in deep shadow beneath the sloping eaves, watched and listened, and I guessed it was Cadmon. Derian stepped through the open doorway and into the darkness of the shed. The sound of clinking chains drifted across to me, then Felix appeared at the door followed by Souk the first mate and Anaxos the navigator. Six slaves followed, hurrying down to the jetty.

Derian hissed at Felix, "I don't want to see you back here again, is that clear? I have spared your life! Never, ever come back!"

Down on the jetty, Felix grasped the tiller. Souk released the ship from its mooring, the slaves pulled hard on the oars, and the ship slipped silently away.

Derian watched in relief as darkness swallowed the ship.

"So, it *was* you!" Cadmon came silently behind Derian and whispered in his ear, Derian squirming as Cadmon's knife pressed against his brother's throat.

"What in hell's name...!" he croaked, hardly daring to draw breath.

"It was you who committed Alric, Tola and me to a living hell on Felix's ship in the middle of winter seven years ago, wasn't it? It was you, who stole from our father to pay Felix to take me out of your miserable life, wasn't it? Now it is you who has released them tonight, so that your iniquity would not be found out come the morning. There's not much left to say, is there?"

Derian's voice was desperate.

"Let me go!"

"Now listen to me, you scum. You are a cheat and a liar, and your day of reckoning will surely come. In the meantime, this will remain secret until Mother and Father have both passed away. Do you understand?"

"Yes!" he choked.

"Judgment Day is not cancelled for you Derian; merely postponed. Now take your horse, and get your fat arse back to Eastringe. To cover your departure, I will say that urgent business has arisen, and you could not stay longer. Now get out of my sight!"

Cadmon released his grip and Derian collapsed on his knees. Cadmon turned on his heel, passing by the circle of eight carts where I knelt, hiding in the dark.

"You can get up now, Alric," Cadmon said, without a glance in my direction.

I rose stiffly to my feet.

"I thought you were going to kill him. You let Derian go," I said accusingly.

Cadmon paused at the entrance to the Hall, the light from the fire flickering on his face as the sound of hoof beats thundered past towards the bridge.

"I cannot expose Derian for what he has done. The disgrace would fall on my parents, who are innocent of all this. It would kill them. No, Alric, I am in this for the long game. When they have both passed away, then it will be the time to expose Derian for what he is."

"And Felix?" I pressed him, appalled by this sudden turn of events. "He gets away without a scratch? Cadmon, we came very, very close to death at sea because of him!"

Cadmon faced me, putting both hands on my shoulders.

"Trust me, Alric. This is no time for revenge. He has a price to pay and he will not escape. Let's count our lucky stars that we're here at all. In the meanwhile, my true brother, come and join the feast!"

III

KING ETHELBERT RATTEBURGH,

April, AD 597

A BLAST FROM the lookout's horn sounded on the pinnacle of the fort, overlooking the broad Wantsum Channel. Inside the Mead Hall, the tension was rising. Sighart rose to his feet. Glancing at Augustinus for a moment, he clasped the Bishop's hand and left the Hall, walking swiftly down to the quay to welcome his King.

Augustinus's calm, reassuring voice broke the silence.

"Stand by, everyone."

The Mead Hall opened out to a view of the old Roman fort to the north, and the Wantsum Channel to the east, so we had no difficulty seeing Ethelbert's warship sweeping towards the fort. This was a good day for a meeting, the sky clear and a gentle but cold breeze ruffling the long grass. It seemed an age before the first spears and helmeted heads appeared, coming up the hill. Ethelbert had chosen to meet under a large oak tree near the south wall of the fort, about a hundred or so yards from the Mead Hall. Two warriors appeared, carrying the King's throne and setting it down in the shade. More chairs and stools soon followed; one for Queen Bertha, two for their sons Eadbald and Ethelwald, and some of the Earls who had accompanied the King from Coningsburh.

A dozen warriors of the King's Guard strode ahead of Ethelbert, their hair long and straggly, faces disappearing under thick beards and long moustaches. Dressed in mail, cloak, tunic and leggings, the Guards also carried swords, painted shields and spears. They stood in a formidable line, directly behind the King's throne.

Queen Bertha and her two sons soon followed. The older son was sixteen years old, the younger fourteen and helped up the path by a warrior on account of a weakness in the young boy's legs. Arriving last, King Ethelbert strode up majestically with an air of confidence, a crown on his head and a heavy gold chain around his neck. I pursed my lips in a silent whistle of admiration as the King took his seat.

Sighart, as host for the occasion, sat to the left of his King. Queen Bertha took her seat to the right of her husband with her two boys, her headdress draped over her shoulders, a small silver crown adorning her brow. The murmur of conversation among the King's retinue gradually subsided, as though about to watch a spectacle begin. The King spoke to Sighart and the Earl signalled to Augustinus and our companions to come forward and greet the King.

The choreography on Augustinus's part had been carefully rehearsed, as Sighart had advised.

"That's good," Laurentius had declared in a crass comment the previous day. "We must be sure to put on a good circus to impress these pagans."

But for once, he was partially right; yes, we *were* good.

*

This was the day we had struggled so long and so hard for, and now the scene was set. Chanting litanies, we processed out of the Mead Hall at a well-measured pace, carrying in front an icon of Christ painted in gold on a board about a foot square.

Augustinus, wearing full episcopal regalia, carried a modest wooden crook. A white and gold-trimmed cloak hung from his shoulders and covered his white vestments, a pointed mitre rested on his tonsured head, adding to his considerable height. Our Bishop came to a halt, standing only yards away from Ethelbert, with everyone else from our party behind him.

In addition to the painted icon, we had brought vestments, metalwork, reliquaries, and books that pointed to the advantages of learning, and a jewelled copy of the four Gospels, scribed and illuminated in Rome. All these we carried in procession by forty of our companions to greet Ethelbert. Our choreography, I knew, was impressive. We were large enough to be an extremely well disciplined war band.

The King was taken by surprise at the spectacle. He turned and spoke to Sighart, and in a moment one of the King's men brought a chair for Augustinus, saying, "The King bids that you and your men sit down."

I repeated this boldly to Augustinus in Latin, while beneath my monastic habit my legs trembled with tension. Bishop Augustinus turned and signalled our company to sit on the grass, then took his seat and waited.

Sighart, called out, "The King bids that you preach to him the good news of life that your message has promised us."

We had prepared for days, Augustinus working on his sermon, draft after draft, while our monks, with Cadmon, Sighart, Wulfrun and I listened carefully and offered suggestions.

Now Augustinus rose to his feet, and like an orator in the ancient Roman Forum, stretched out a hand to speak.

The day, the hour, the minute, the moment had finally come.

*

"I bring you greetings, King Ethelbert, from His Holiness Pope Gregorius in Rome, who has sent us to bring Good News to you and the people of your Kingdom of Cantia. We are here at the behest of our Pope, who foresees that the state of this world will not long endure the ravages of war and earthquakes, plagues, famine and disasters, that everywhere assail us."

Augustinus paused while I translated. The King briefly nodded for the Bishop to continue, watching his demeanour, observing his expression, tone and sincerity of voice, and listening attentively to the Saxon translation.

"Half of our companions who sit here before you are from Rome. The other half have come from Turones in Francia, followers of the teachings of Bishop Martinus, formerly of that city."

Queen Bertha, surprised at the unexpected mention of her former city where she had lived in exile, leaned forward with great attention.

Augustinus continued. "As a gesture of our sincerity and commitment to you, we have brought with us practical tools and medicines." He gestured behind him to the eight heavy-laden carts we had brought this great distance from Rome, and at great cost.

"Also, we bring skills in writing and keeping records that would be helpful to you, O King, in the administration of your Kingdom."

The King nodded approval again.

"However, above all else, we have come with a message of God who so loved the world that he sent his only Son, to set us free from the fear and power of demons, spirits and idols. Everyone who puts his life in the hands of the Son of God will have eternal life. For this reason, O king, we have come to bring this message to your Kingdom also. Now, if I may, I shall share with you a story!"

A shuffle of anticipation rippled through the King's companions.

Augustinus began telling the tale of a babe who was born by a miracle to a woman called Maria, in the cold heart of winter, and in a faraway land...

*

Augustinus spoke for several minutes. In the long, silent moments that followed, the very air seemed to hold its breath. I looked at the faces of the King's warriors standing in the second row, their muscular arms folded, festooned with gold armbands studded with jewels, eyes watchful and expressionless.

The outcome of our mission now rested entirely on King Ethelbert's response.

The King sat long in thought, his gaze fixed on a patch of grass a few yards away, where Theodore stood holding the processional cross.

At last, with his mind resolved, the King looked up.

"Your words and promises are well-spoken Bishop!" he exclaimed.

I let out my breath, the tension within me draining away.

"However, because these things you have said are new to our people, and we are uncertain of their meaning and their promises, I cannot so easily consent to them, and forsake what our Saxon people have for so long adhered to."

Whether King Ethelbert spoke for himself, or on behalf of his Earls and the King's Guard, I could not tell. Ethelbert and Bertha had been married for nearly two decades. Ethelbert understood a great deal about his Queen's traditions in the Catholic Faith, so that what Augustinus had said did not come as something new to him. However, beyond the narrow circle of maids attending to the Queen, there were very few who had any knowledge of the Christ, and Ethelbert's response seemed to offer little hope for our mission.

I silently groaned. Despite all our preparations and Augustinus's oratory, we had failed. Our carts stood ready and packed, we could be sent back on the morrow. Failure is an orphan, and without supporters and the backing of the King, we would be left at the mercy of strangers at every place we dared to lay our heads. Cadmon, Tola and I, being Saxon, could remain here if we so wished; but our companions would face a long and arduous journey, lasting many more months to return home.

Ethelbert continued, "But, because you have come from afar as strangers to my Kingdom, and you desire to share with us those things you believe to be true and greatly beneficial, you have my word as King that we intend you no harm. Therefore, I grant you a place in my Royal Hall, and I will also supply you with all the things necessary for your sustenance. Nor do we forbid you to preach, so that you may gather as many as you can to your religion!"

Ethelbert's gesture was overwhelmingly generous. When I had finished translating the King's words, a sigh of relief escaped from our companions behind us. What seemed hopeless only a moment ago now took on a very different complexion. Also, Ethelbert's response to Augustinus was exceedingly canny—in a sentence, he had bought time to make the transition he and Bertha had waited for so long, from pagan warlord to Christian monarch. And yet, at the same time, he would not alienate his people by rejecting their age-old values and traditions—and their adherence to Wodin.

Ethelbert sat back on his throne, the atmosphere now more relaxed, friendly and enquiring.

"Now, tell us, what is it you bring us that is of practical benefit? You have challenged us concerning our gods, but what of the lives of mortal men? You are from Rome, and we know also something about the splendours of Constantinople. What have you brought that has practical value to those who labour on the land?"

"My Lord," I translated in response, "you mention the splendours of Rome and Constantinople. We bring these gifts for your Kingdom." Augustinus turned and gestured to our lay brothers arrayed behind him.

"We have come bringing skilled men who can increase your harvests, and herbs and ointments to heal the sick. We will teach the skills of reading and writing to whoever you choose from among your people—and in your own tongue—so that your laws can be written down for all to see. And also for your officials who have oversight of your great estates, so that they may keep a record of your harvests and your livestock, your cattle and your sheep and goats, indeed, of all your property. In short, King Ethelbert, we have come to share all this with you, so that you too may have the skills and the knowledge to do what others have done elsewhere to make their kingdoms prosper, in the name of the one true God."

Ethelbert was more than interested; the gifts of knowledge and tools that Augustinus had brought from Rome were beyond price. Augustinus bowed, and a vista of possibilities began to open before the King.

But a nagging doubt remained—would the King *really* overcome his reluctance in surrendering old gods for new? Would these 'gifts' as Augustinus had described them, be sufficient to overcome the opposition of Ethelbert's Earls and leading men? Not least, how would the pagan High Priest of Wodin react? He was not present at this meeting.

The King leaned forward on his throne, his gaze falling on me with an encouraging smile.

"And you are?"

"My name is Alric, my Lord."

"Alric, you have come here from Rome, have you not? Tell me, how is it that you speak our mother tongue so fluently?"

I inflated my chest just a little.

"I am a Saxon by birth, my Lord! I was born here in Ratteburg, seventeen years ago." I turned, pointing to the very spot; a grassy knoll less than a hundred paces from the King's throne.

"My father is Galen, my mother Erlina, and they live at the Haven." I pointed across the grey waters of the estuary to Sandwic Haven.

"Your Queen was present at my birth on the day she first set foot in Cantia, and gave me a gold coin that I still carry with me to this day."

Queen Bertha turned and whispered to the King. Ethelbert nodded, and she turned to me.

"Come forward, please, Alric." She gestured for me to kneel on the grass before her.

"May I see your gold coin?"

From my pocket I fished out a coin attached to a leather cord, and held it out to her. The Queen examined it closely before handing it back.

"Yes, this is the one. I hope I shan't have to give this back to you again, Alric! Who knows where it might take you next?"

"I pray it will keep me here, my Lady."

The Queen smiled and nodded. She gestured, and I stood up and continued my story.

"At the age of nearly ten years, I took a boatload of fish to Raculf with my father, for Modranicht, where your father King Eormenric, my Lord, drew his last breath. My friend Cadmon and I," gesturing towards Cadmon standing alongside his warhorse, "discovered a hoard of spears that Earl Hrothgar of Tanet had hidden in the old Roman fort, near Raculf. And on the following day, you defeated the Earl in combat on the beach, and exiled him with his son to Francia."

The King leaned even further forward stroking his chin, and nodded.

"My Kingdom certainly lay in the balance that day! Go on, lad, go on."

"Early the next morning Cadmon, my sister Tola and I were seized by slavers at Sandwic Haven. Tola was later sold in Francia as a chambermaid. She served Queen Ingoberga in Turones to the end."

At the mention of her mother, the Queen conferred briefly with her husband again.

"Your sister Tola, Alric. Is she here too?"

She is, my Lady!"

The atmosphere had begun to take on the happy atmosphere of a market festival.

The Queen commanded, "Then let her come forward!"

Odelinda had spent most of the morning dressing Tola for this occasion. Although I was her brother, I too found myself speechless as she came forward. Tola, like a princess, wore a white linen habit and a dark green cloak over her shoulders, her headdress ringed with tiny yellow flowers. Tola picked her way between the rows of our companions to stand next to me, and the onlookers drew in their breath.

"You are Tola?" the Queen inquired.

"I am, Your Majesty," she replied softly but clearly, standing boldly upright.

"You were a handmaid to my mother, Queen Ingoberga, in Turones?"

"I was, Your Majesty, in the castle on the river."

Bertha nodded, remembering well both the castle and the city.

"You were with her in her last moments?"

"I was at her bedside to the end, my Lady. She had a peaceful ending. I was privileged to be with her in her last moments on this earth."

"I am most reassured by this, my child. Thank you."

The Queen paused, clearly moved.

"And what is it that occupies you, now that you have returned to us?"

"I am a trained herbalist, my Lady." Tola's eyes flicked briefly to the Queen's youngest son, a momentary glance that was not lost on the Queen.

She said, "You must come and visit me at Coningsburh soon, Tola, so that I can hear all your story—and learn about your herbs and potions too."

Tola curtseyed, and Ethelbert addressed Augustinus again.

"You have spoken well this day, Bishop. You have brought good cheer and hope for the future! I am especially grateful that you have brought home these three youngsters who were taken from my Kingdom. So doubly I say yes, you are welcome to enter our Kingdom under my protection as my guests. Let everyone know this," he said, briefly looking around at his nobles and warriors. "*No one will bring you harm; you have my word, and let it be known to all.*

As for me, I must weigh up what you have said, and I shall speak again with you concerning your God, at another time."

Ethelbert stood up abruptly, signalling the end of the day's proceedings. He paused briefly and gestured to Cadmon.

"Cadmon, we have yet to hear your tale, which you will tell us in my Hall tonight. Follow us to Coningsburh, where all of you shall have a place in our Royal Hall. Now," he called out, "to the ships!"

IV

CONINGSBURH THE KING'S FORT

April, AD 597

WE LOADED OUR carts onto Sighart's ship and pulled away from the quay into the Channel, heading westwards to the shipyard-cum-trading port of Fordwic.

Earl Sighart put a hand on Augustinus's shoulder.

"By nature, I am a practical man, Bishop," Sighart confided. "I have seen, over these last few days, that you have made a man of Cadmon, and he returns to us with an unblemished reputation for his fighting prowess. But also, you have performed a miracle by bringing him safely home. For this, I have nothing but gratitude! Wodin, Loki, Thunor, Tiw…the gods all stood by and did nothing to prevent my son's capture, nor aid his return. *Nothing!* From today, you can count on me as one of your firmest supporters—I want to follow in the steps of the Christ that you have spoken of today."

The two men clasped hands. An ally such as Sighart was not to be taken lightly, and Augustinus suggested they might make preparations for his baptism.

Augustinus addressed our companions, reflecting on this eventful day and its outcome. "You have done well, all of you," he called out. "I could not have hoped for more. King Ethelbert seemed eager to engage with the mission, and he sees the benefits, both spiritual and material."

Wulfrun added, "I believe Ethelbert also knows that Christian kingdoms are more prosperous than pagan ones." We nodded agreement, but Laurentius was predictably cautious. He said, "At least, we have come when the Franks would not, which tells us everything about the dismal state of the Frankish Church! Bishop Letardus, Queen Bertha's chaplain, passed away last year. But King Ethelbert will need to proceed with great care, even though his warriors all but worship him."

"They have waited seven years since Queen Bertha requested a mission," Petrus reminded us. "I think the King realises time is running out for new religious practices to make an impression on his people. I can see that the King desires to make himself more than a war leader. And for this, he needs men around him who are literate—and those of the Faith."

Two hours later we landed at Fordwic and unloaded our carts for the journey along the muddy, ancient Saxon Way to Coningsburh. Dusk began to overtake us as we reached our goal. Queen Bertha had already allocated several wood-and-thatch buildings for us, near to her Chapel, but away from the everyday business of the King's compound. The time had come to put behind us any thought of returning to Rome or Turones. Within the hour, we stood ready to enter King Ethelbert's Royal Hall.

Earl Sighart briefed us before we entered.

"Men of highest status sit closest to the King. Other experienced warriors sit closest to the Queen. Younger men and less-noble guests sit along the opposite wall, with the long open fire between. The task of seating forty of you will fall to the King's Steward, so I can't say where everyone will be seated. The Steward will greet you at the door and lead you to your places. Follow him. Usually, only men are welcomed here, except for occasional appearances of the Queen and her maidens. Also, the King welcomes travellers seeking lodgings for the night, and traders and peddlers who come with goods and services to offer. Of course, wandering storytellers and minstrels always enliven an evening. And the King will want to hear Cadmon's story for himself!"

Speaking to Augustinus, Earl Sighart said, "You mentioned you have brought gifts for the King and Queen. May I advise you to exercise caution here? Our time-honoured practice is that the King is the giver of gifts for his people, not the other way round. The gift-giver is always a person of higher status; so do not give anything to the King by way of a gift, unless he first gives a gift to you. But because you come as an emissary from the Pope in Rome, King Ethelbert will receive the gift. He will acknowledge your Pope Gregorius as everyone would acknowledge the Emperor."

We entered a spacious porch leading into the King's Hall, overwhelmed by the sight that greeted us. Way above our heads, a forest of oak-beams soared into the darkness; lamps, fixed to stout and intricately carved oak columns, illuminated the dark interior. Candles burned brightly on tables set along the walls. Bearskins and warrior shields decorated the Hall as reminders of great men and past glories.

A haze of smoke hung over the Hall. We crossed the floor of pounded earth-and-straw towards a large, rectangular sunken fire pit, glowing in the centre. Smoke escaped through a hole in the high, thatched roof, and the smell of roast boar's meat greeted our nostrils. The focal point was not the smouldering fire but the high table, raised on a dais to provide the King with a view of everyone in the Hall. Exquisitely carved, high-backed chairs awaited Ethelbert and his Queen. Those who sat furthest from the King were 'bench-sitters' not nobles, and ale, not mead, was supplied in abundance.

The Hall was filling rapidly as we arrived. Four of the King's six Earls sat close to the throne. Sighart briefly acknowledged them, finding it hard to hear above the babble of conversations. He explained to Augustinus as he took his seat: "These are Ethelbert's closest advisers who ensure that the King's laws are enforced in each of their territories in the Kingdom of Cantia. In addition to the Earls, you can see some of their lower-ranking Thanes further down the tables. These are warriors who defend the King in war, collect duties, repair fortifications, guard tax collectors, and maintain bridges and even some of the old Roman roads. The Thanes owe fealty to their Earls, and make up the core of the *fyrd*, the army, in times of war."

Most of the King's men of rank were already seated and drinking heavily. Boars' heads decorated the long tables, a token of the meal to follow. Special tableware marked the significance of this occasion: drinking-horns, glamorous vessels, cups bound by metal, glass beakers and goblets. Behind the King's table, large woven panels displayed the skills and successes of the Kingdom, and also kept-out the night chill.

This awesome site was the gathering place for the King's warriors, a sanctuary where they drank mead and beer, celebrated past victories, and heard tales of bravery passed down the generations. Above all else, the Hall lay at the heart of our Saxon culture. This was King Ethelbert's Court; here his word was final, his laws made and enforced; and here also, most future Kings were chosen. Most of Ethelbert's commercial business was conducted here, judgments pronounced, justice dispensed, contracts made and dissolved; and here too, all praiseworthy deeds began and ended.

Everyone rose to loud shouts and raised goblets as Ethelbert and Bertha, now with Tola by her side, swept majestically into the Hall. The King remained standing as he addressed the gathering.

"Men of Cantia, we have the honour of welcoming Bishop Augustinus and his companions, some sent from the Pope in Rome, and others from the Kingdoms of Francia! They have come to tell us of the Christian God who is worshipped in many parts of the world, including Francia, the home of my wedded wife! I know that you will extend to our guests the courtesy due to high-ranking officials from another land. Enjoy!"

All faces turned towards us as hands, mugs and knives hammered on the tables, accompanied by loud shouts of welcome. Augustinus was seated opposite the King at his table. As I was their translator, I sat to our Bishop's left, opposite Queen Bertha and noted that her fine garments could only have been woven in Francia, or perhaps even Constantinople. Earl Sighart sat next to the King, gleaning what he could from the meeting at Ratteburg earlier in the day, and conferring with Augustinus.

Next to Sighart sat Coifin, the High Priest of Wodin. Laurentius and Wulfrun, Petrus and the remainder of our monks sat further along the table. Our lay brothers and the Frankish contingent from

Turones sat together at tables along the far wall, on the far side of the fire. Food was brought immediately to the King, followed by all the tables, in order of priority. Pork, bread, fruit, beer and mead began to flow freely into the night.

Queen Bertha turned to Tola. "I shall send for you to come to me soon, Tola. I must hear the story of my mother's last days in Turones. It would mean so much to me."

Ethelbert arose from his throne, known also as his gift-stool, the source of bounty in the form of rewards for deeds well done. Tokens would be given later in the form of badges of merit, rings, coins, armbands or necklaces fashioned in gold and precious jewels. Now, an almost sacred moment of silence began to descend on the Hall.

The King's Steward emerged from the antechamber with two of the King's warriors, carrying a heavy jewelled box between them, which they placed on the table before the King. Ethelbert took a key from his pocket and unlocked the lid.

What the King said and did next would be vitally important for the future of the mission.

As Earl Sighart had explained, a well-worn protocol existed around the giving and receiving of gifts. A crackle of tension passed through my companions and those behind us across the King's Hall as Ethelbert opened the lid of his treasure-hoard. These gifts bound the receiver in a new relationship of obligation. What obligation, I wondered, would this place Augustinus under?

Ethelbert reached into his gift-box and withdrew a gold necklace, holding it high. It was a finely worked gold and bronze cross with a ruby centre. "I know this is the symbol of your religion, and I give it to you as a token of your ministry among us."

Augustinus now rose to his feet. "King Ethelbert, I greatly appreciate your gift, which I shall receive on behalf of our Pope, and believe we shall be fruitful in our endeavours amongst your people. I too have a gift for you, from Pope Gregorius of Rome!"

Augustinus presented the King with a dark purple cloak of heavy woollen weave, and a clasp of a gold deer at the throat. To Queen Bertha, he gave a cross set in a circular gold disk, finely tooled and produced in Turones. Both King and Queen were delighted; with these gifts, Augustinus had overcome the problem of gift-giver and recipient by receiving the gifts in the name of the Pope.

The King signalled to Cadmon to stand, and turning to me he said, "Alric, did you not say, without Cadmon's military prowess on our way here through Francia, I can truly witness that none of us would be alive this day?"

"I did, my Lord."

"And Cadmon, you are Earl Sighart's son, of whom Alric speaks?"

"I am, my Lord."

"Now, it is not our way in this Hall to boast of our own deeds while there are others at hand, and unhindered by false modesty, who can better tell the tale! That is the task of the bard with his songs, is it not?" The King turned to me. "Therefore, Alric, will you tell us some of Cadmon's exploits, so that we may know the measure of this man!"

I cleared my throat nervously, glanced around at the eagerly waiting crowd of guests, and plunged in, putting everything I had into it, embellishing where needed, skimming over where not.

Everyone strained forward to catch every word, exchanging glances as each heroic adventure followed another until one last tale remained to be told.

I said, "Lastly, my Lord, you might want to hear the fate of Hrothgar, formerly Earl of Tanet, and his son Falk, both of whom you sent into exile in Francia. But I was not a witness to these events. Cadmon was!"

The king turned in surprise to Cadmon. "Has Earl Hrothgar met his end? Come! Tell us, Cadmon; tell us now, in your own words!"

I sat down as Cadmon rose to speak, and here in the Royal Hall sat the first audience ever to hear his story. Cadmon delivered his account as he would to the Commander of his Roman Garrison: brief, factual and informative.

He began, "As our expedition from Rome under Bishop Augustinus arrived at the annual Marchfields Gathering, which is held each year a few miles outside Parisius where Queen Bertha was born, the young King Chlothar conscripted me to join in the battle he had planned against the King of Austrasia. To my surprise, both Hrothgar and his son Falk were given the leadership of this battle. We set off in the early morning, and I travelled some of the time with Hrothgar, and at others with his Cavalry.

"Hrothgar was only interested in me as a trophy, but Falk his son was more inquisitive. He would ask, 'Where did you join the Cavalry? What was it like? Where do you come from?' Falk spoke no Latin, and I could not let him know I spoke Saxon, so we used a Frankish translator. I think Falk was suspicious if not downright resentful of me; he would look at me sideways, trying to make up his mind where he might have seen me before. But that was too long ago, and I was much younger—a boy, certainly, and not yet a man. On that first day, we covered about twenty-five miles, as Hrothgar was intent on getting to his destination with speed, so he could take the Austrasian troops by surprise."

The King pressed for more detail.

"And where did you spend the night?"

"In a castrum, my Lord, a fortified town called Civitas Silvanectium, surrounded by a seven-foot-high stone wall. The locals call it Senlis," Cadmon added, turning to the Queen. Bertha leaned forward, smiling and nodding at this bit of news of the Kingdom of Neustria. Her recently deceased chaplain, Bishop Letardus, had come from Senlis, accompanying Bertha to Cantia as her Chaplain.

Cadmon pressed on.

"The next day, a battle commenced between the Frankish kingdoms of Austrasia and Neustria. During our charge, as I drew near, I saw that Hrothgar had fallen from his horse."

"Oh?" Ethelbert interrupted. "How so?"

" I believe he suffered a seizure of the heart, my Lord."

Ethelbert was puzzled. "From what cause?"

"When I presented my true identity to him, it seems that he did not die in combat, but of a weak heart condition. I was unable to mark his passing to the Great Mead Hall of Wodin by our tradition of placing his axe in his hand. He died in the midst of battle; but alas, not because of it."

A moment's silence followed, as everyone pictured the scene. All of us present that night knew Hrothgar had challenged Ethelbert for the Crown of the Kingdom of Cantia, and he had failed. A titter of laughter began to spread around the Hall.

"Ah", said the King with some attempt at sympathy, "That is unfortunate. I understand the position you found yourself in, Cadmon. But what of his son, Falk?"

"Alas, my Lord, he too fell on the battlefield."

Several of the warriors, who had known Falk for the coward he was, laughed out loud.

Ethelbert seemed shocked. "How so? What was the manner of his passing?"

"It occurred in that same battle charge, my Lord. He died with an arrow—in his back."

Ethelbert shook his head. "Regrettably, an arrow in the back seems to run in the family!"

Everyone knew that several years earlier, Hrothgar's older brother had died fleeing from the line of battle. The assembly burst into raucous laughter all around us; banging on the tables, the warriors pouring beer on one another's heads, and eyes wet with tears.

At last, the noise abated, and Ethelbert addressed Cadmon again.

"You vouch that this is true?"

"I do, my Lord. And I have brought back with me a token as evidence."

Cadmon gestured to our Bishop.

Augustinus rose to his feet and laid a thin, wooden box in Queen Bertha's hands.

"Your Majesty, we bring you a relic that Cadmon rescued from this battle—one of the rarest relics in Francia that anyone could ever wish to behold!"

In the expectant silence that followed, all necks craned forward as the Queen, her expression puzzled, opened the clips and carefully raised the lid of the box. For a long moment Bertha stared at the ancient, faded and threadbare red cloak, and very, very carefully lifted it up for all to see.

Augustinus explained, "This is the missing half of the cloak that San Martinus of Turones gave to a beggar as he sat shivering at the gates of Cabillonum many years ago. During this battle of Hrothgar's, the Chaplain was struck down, and Cadmon came upon him moments after he fell. One half of the cloak is held in the Abbey of San Martinus in Turones; all our companions from Rome and Turones bear witness to it. But we give *this* half to you, my Lady— perhaps for a shrine in your chapel of San Martinus?"

Bertha held the ancient, threadbare cloak in her hands, her face expressing shock and amazement. All eyes turned to Ethelbert sitting beside her. The King grasped at once what this meant to his Queen and hammered his approval on the table, the sound growing louder and louder all around the Hall.

The Queen wiped her tears, graciously expressed her thanks, and carefully returned the cloak to its box.

"This relic of San Martinus *will* have pride of place as a shrine in our San Martinus chapel," she managed to say, as more shouts rang out all around the Hall.

The King called for silence and declared, "Cadmon, you have done your King and our people a great service. Come forward. I have a gift in recognition of your skill, your persistence, and your bravery in the face of danger during your journey, and in returning home to us!"

From his large carved gift box, Ethelbert drew out a magnificent engraved silver and gold armband, presenting it to Cadmon saying, "To a son of Cantia, who has performed exceptionally in his commission from the Pope, to bring both family and friends safely to our shores!"

Shouts of approval burst out again around the Hall.

*

Cadmon had made his mark. To rousing applause, Queen Bertha and Tola withdrew from the Hall. The adulation for the Queen was much more than politeness; the warriors held their Queen in the highest esteem. So did we. As she departed, I raised my glass in salute to her, and caught Cadmon's eye. He nodded in return. Yes, the Queen was a very fine woman indeed!

Coifin the High Priest had remained silent for much of the evening. Now, unable to contain his anger, he leaned across Sighart to address the King.

"My Lord, I was not informed of your meeting earlier today. I fear that you have invited a viper into your camp! We may all rue this day that you opened your table to these *outlanders*!"

Ethelbert took a few moments before replying, holding back his anger with an enormous effort of will.

"Coifin, a King must deal with all manner of people, whether we agree with them or not, whether we approve of their ways of life or not—all for the sake of the peace and prosperity of the Kingdom that I have inherited from my forebears. Half of those 'vipers,' as you call them, have come to us from Francia. They hail from the place where my Queen was born and lived before our marriage. Would it not be churlish of me to refuse hospitality to such a group, or to turn a deaf ear to the message from the Pope in Rome himself, asking me to receive those missionaries whom he has personally entrusted to us?"

Red-faced with anger, Coifin made his excuses and left the Hall.

A feeling of doom crept into my stomach.

Here, I reckoned, was the one who really could thwart our mission to Cantia.

V

OESTRE CHAPEL OF SAN MARTINUS,

April, AD 597

IT WAS THOR'S Day, in pagan terms; and three days before Oestre, or Easter in the Church's Calendar. During the night, the rain had fallen on the King's fortress of Coningsburh and the surrounding countryside. I squelched on the path with every step as thick mud sucked at my sandals. Greeting the guard, I asked if I might climb up to look at the view over the wall. From here, lookouts could see anyone coming from miles away. Built on the brow of a steep hill overlooking an abandoned Roman town, Ethelbert's fortified village was surrounded by a vast, defensive wooden stockade. The Royal Hall and apartments dominated the centre of this compound, and a wood fence kept out chickens, dogs and pigs.

We fell into conversation as the guard slowly paced back and forth on a raised walkway of stone and dried mud, circling the perimeter. Like all Ethelbert's guards, he bore a shield and a spear with a sword hanging from his belt, and a thick cloak over his shoulders keeping out the chilly morning dew. He was happy to talk and break the monotony of patrolling the wall and paused, following my gaze. Down in the valley green shoots of spring were evident but little else, not even the Roman ruins of the ancient town.

"Hardly anyone has lived there since our Saxon people came," the watchman explained. "All that's left is the wall and one or two old buildings. Everything else lies buried beneath the earth."

I looked down towards the south. Fifty or so yards below us a Chapel of red Roman brick and local grey stone stood out among a few scattered trees.

"That's the Chapel of San Martinus," he said, as a solitary bell began to toll. I thanked the guard, and hurried down for Morning Prayer.

Afterwards, as we walked back to Coningsburh, Queen Bertha spoke to Tola about her knowledge of herbs.

"Tola, it did not escape my notice when we spoke at Ratteburg yesterday that your eyes turned to my son, Ethelwald. That set me wondering. Do you perhaps know of any medication that might help to strengthen his limbs?"

Tola nodded. "I have brought a small bottle with me, your Majesty. The taste is a little bitter, but it quickly passes. A spoonful twice a day could help. And massaging his legs with a salve would be good for him. I will give you that too."

Tola handed a small basket to the Queen.

"Thank you, Tola. I'll begin his treatment at once!"

*

Three days later, we gathered again in the Chapel dedicated to San Martinus for the Resurrection Celebration, and on this occasion Ethelbert accompanied Bertha and their two sons to the Easter service. Augustinus rose to preach his first sermon in the chapel, speaking of the miracle of resurrection of the crucified Christ.

Ethelbert remained seated as Bertha approached the altar with her two young princes. Ethelwald, supported by his mother and older brother, walked with difficulty. They knelt at the altar, Bertha holding out her hand to receive the consecrated bread. Augustinus paused, looking searchingly at Ethelwald; then, putting his hands on the boy's head, he prayed. Having received the bread, Bertha stood up and helped her son to his feet. Ethelwald hesitated for a moment, then let go of his mother's hand, stood unaided and took a few small steps forward. Bertha grasped his hand, and he walked a few more steps. Then a few more, until they arrived at his seat next to his father King Ethelbert.

At the altar Laurentius, holding a chalice, turned to the Bishop and hissed through gritted teeth in Augustinus's ear.

"Well, Bishop, what was that all about? Are we in the magic business, now?"

Ethelbert sat watching, looking stony-faced, and left without a word immediately after Mass.

*

The following morning, as we left the chapel after daily prayers, a messenger arrived from the King. Augustinus read the letter, written in Bertha's hand, and the two of us hurried over to the King's quarters in the Royal Hall. My heart was pounding. What reaction would the King have to Augustinus, praying for Ethelwald's healing? In our Saxon Kingdom, magicians haunted the religious underworld, part-sorcerers, part fortune-tellers and part medicine-healers. Saxons, like the Frankish peasantry and some of their nobility, were deeply interested in magic, but from the outset the Church had set its face against the practice of it.

Queen Bertha remained seated, expressionless as we entered the anteroom to the King's chambers. Ethelbert was restless as he paced the room. Without inviting us to sit, the King came straight to the point, his voice raised to the point of anger.

"What did you do to my son yesterday, Bishop?" he demanded. The Bishop opened his mouth to speak, but Ethelbert spoke on. "I have never seen the like of this before! When Ethelwald was born with a problem in his legs, I believed I had somehow angered Wodin. And my Queen thought that her God was angry because she had married a pagan! So, last night I feared that your effect on him might have passed like a dream. But when he awoke, he seemed as well as ever! I have seen magic performed many times—by Coifin, the High Priest, witches and others too—but never the healing of a body like this!"

In a calmer voice, Ethelbert came to the point. "How do I follow your Christ, Bishop? However difficult it may be, what must I do?"

Augustinus remained silent for a few moments, taken by surprise at this sudden change of events. He replied, "Whoever calls on the name of the Lord will be saved. That is the promise of God. You have asked, 'What should I do'? That is your answer. The outward sign of your belief through baptism follows an inner change in your life, which is faith."

"I believe, Bishop! But I am also ignorant. You will teach me, so I can be baptised."

Bertha, unable to hold back the tears, broke into sobs. After seventeen years, this may have been the most significant moment of their married life together. Ethelbert sat down beside his wife, placing a comforting hand on hers.

"My Queen has been so patient with me!" he said with surprising tenderness. "I owe her this. Now, Bishop, when shall I be baptised?"

After a few minutes brief discussion, the date for Ethelbert's baptism was set for Pentecost, in the Year of Our Lord, 597.

*

As we hurried away I asked Augustinus, "Is that why you were so anxious to reach Cantia in time for Easter? Were you expecting something like this might happen?"

"Right from the beginning, Alric, I experienced a strong urge that we must be here in time for Easter. I did not know why, or how, or for what reason; only that at one stage in our journey through Francia—when we left Turones, in fact—I knew we must take the shortest and fastest route, even though it seemed most likely to lead us towards danger. Now I know why. The danger lay in what seemed the safer route through Reims. Had we taken it ..." Augustinus shuddered. "None of us Alric, least of all Ethelbert himself, expected events to unfold this quickly. As you can see, Ethelbert's kinsmen worship him; but even so, he has to move in harmony with his nobles if he wants to address the broader implications of change."

With the morning events swirling around in my head, I sat at one of the tables in the King's empty Hall to write up my notes of the meeting. As I worked on the manuscript, I overheard the voices of two men approaching the open door. The King's voice was unmistakable.

"I tell you in confidence, this has been neither a sudden nor an easy decision. I have long searched for some tangible reason to change my mind, but my people have bowed to our gods for untold centuries."

"Well, my King, why do you forsake them now?"

"Why? Because at last, I do have something tangible; my own younger son."

"Ethelwald?"

"The same! You know how much he has suffered since birth. Neither Coifin the High Priest, nor the witches and soothsayers, have healed him. The Wyrd sisters, they say, have chosen his fate. Charlatans! A few days ago, Tola gave my Queen some herbal drink for my son, and yesterday, in the chapel of San Martinus, the Bishop put his hands on my son's head and prayed for him. His legs have strengthened, and his progress continues. He is not fully healed, but I have never seen the like of this before! Bishop Augustinus is a miracle-worker who serves his God, not his fortune."

After a pause Ethelbert added, "I will not compel any of my noblemen to abandon the gods of old. Each one must make up his mind. Yes, we respect our ancestors, those great heroes of our past, and their odes of bravery handed down to us. Our tradition is rich with magic and poetry. Our whole way of life is bound up in these beliefs, so that ideas are hard to change, folk-memory is stubborn, and the mind of man prefers the security of tradition to the uncertainty of the new! No, we cannot easily abandon them; but I know for myself that I must."

*

That night I took from my pocket a letter to Paulina I had written in a quiet moment at Ratteburg. I carefully opened it and read my unsent message to her, the only way I could keep the flame alive.

"My dearest Paulina, it seems unnecessary to write that I miss you terribly, but I'll say it anyway. There is an ache in my heart and a gaping hole in my life. Every step has taken me further away from you on our long, long journey through the cities and Kingdoms of Francia.

We have found friends and supporters here, but this is also a dangerous place and we don't always know whom we can trust, or what their motives are. The world is broken, not only in Rome, but also here.

I pray that the message we bring of a Peaceable Kingdom will soon root itself in my native soil, just as your saplings in your orchard in Rome take root and produce fruit at the convent. Perhaps I speak the language of youth, even as I long for wisdom!

My inner call to this venture is the only thing that draws me away from you my dearest, yet my fervent hope is that we may meet again! But now, the Pope's vision is at last unfolding, and I feel that we are called to follow our allotted task.

Ever your beloved Alric."

I longed for Paulina to receive my letter, but I knew of no way I could send it to her. I folded the letter again, carefully slipping it back into my pocket.

VI

SOMETHING OF VALUE CONINGSBURH

April, AD 597

QUEEN BERTHA GESTURED to one of her maids, "Refreshments for our guests, please Marta!"

Tola, Cadmon and I had come at the summons of the Queen to her private chambers. She smiled warmly, "I know that you three have remarkable stories to tell! That is why I have called you together. It seems best to hear from all of you together."

So began a long afternoon with no sense of time passing, as each of us gave an account of our seven years away from home. When my turn came, there was one part of my story that I had hesitated to tell, but Bertha wanted to hear everything.

"Well, my Lady, I can recall my worst moment at sea, a month or so after we were taken into slavery on Felix's ship."

I swallowed hard as my feeling of nausea returned with the memory of huge winds torn and freezing cold waves.

"Tola had been taken from us several days earlier, and in that great and cruel storm I found myself beyond all fear, seeking nothing but revenge for what Felix the skipper had done to us, even if it was at the cost of my own life. I looked at Cadmon who rowed next to me, and despite his great strength and determination, I was certain that this journey, this day, would be our last."

I sat silent, uncertain how I should tell the remainder of this event. Bertha leaned forward, her eyes unwavering, giving me her full attention and urging me to go on.

"It was then that a most remarkable and unexpected vision appeared. My Lady, I know how this must sound, but I saw you holding Tola's hand, both of you as white as wraiths, coming towards our ship, and walking on the waves..." I paused, returning to that moment, so powerful and so deeply painful that I found it difficult to speak.

After a few moments I recovered my composure. "And, you held in your hand the gold coin you had given me at my birth—the same coin I showed to you at Ratteburg. I had worn it every day of my life until we were taken into slavery, and Felix snatched it from my neck."

All the while, as she listened intently, Bertha's eyes had not left my face.

"Please continue," she urged gently.

I took another deep breath.

"I turned away from you and Tola, and looked at Felix, holding a steering oar in his hands. His jerkin was open at the neck, but the coin had gone! I blinked and wiped my eyes and looked back at you, and there was the coin still on the gold chain, held in your hand!"

The Queen smiled as though she already knew what would happen.

"And you have it with you? Show me again, Alric."

I withdrew the coin on its leather cord from my habit pocket. Bertha reached out and carefully took it from me, holding it by the cord as she examined it again.

"Alric, I don't think you ever knew that this coin was minted in Parisius at the time of my birth? Indeed, *for* the day of my birth! Do you see my father's face on it? And his inscription, Charibertus Rex?"

Her face became sad.

"In truth, his standing amongst his brothers and his noblemen in Neustria was extremely poor indeed. But I was his first child, and somehow there was always a strong bond between us. The day that I first arrived at Ratteburg from Francia, I was nervous, even though

I also looked forward enormously to coming to Cantia to marry the dashing young Prince Ethelbert! Then, soon after we landed, one of my maidens told me that a babe had been born to the mother of a churl from Sandwic Haven. I took it as a sign that somehow all would be well for me. And from that moment when I gathered you in my arms, I felt that there was something very special about you."

I looked away, my cheeks burning in embarrassment.

Tola and Cadmon glanced at each other.

Bertha returned my coin, pressing it gently into my palm.

"I have prayed for you every day since your birth, Alric—even though almost ten years passed before I set eyes on you again, on that fateful day at Raculf when Prince Ethelbert overcame Hrothgar, and took up the mantle of King. The following day you were gone, snatched away with Tola and Cadmon. When we learned what had happened, the King sent out a ship to find you—as your father did also, Cadmon. But by the time they reached the shores of Francia, your slaver's ship had come and gone! It was hopeless. Our ships returned home, not knowing what had happened, or whether you were even alive. After this, I took one of my father's gold coins, like the one I gave you, Alric, and hung it around *my* neck as a daily reminder in my prayers for all three of you. Then one day I had a dark sense of unease as I prayed, a feeling of urgency, of danger."

The Queen instinctively reached out and took Tola's hand, re-living that moment.

"With my eyes shut, I held the coin tightly in one hand, and in my mind's eye, Tola, I held you tight, believing that you, at least, were safe. Together we walked towards a ship struggling against towering waves. I saw you Alric, and Cadmon alongside you, soaking wet and cold. I held up my coin as a sign. You have described what transpired next, Alric. Somehow, a connection was made, and both you and I felt that this wasn't the end. So now, your new future awaits!"

*

We left the Queen's chambers, thoughtful and deeply moved, and paused for a while as we looked across the valley below. Tola was the first to break the silence.

"This seems strange, but after what we shared with the Queen this afternoon, I feel that somehow I've recovered some of those lost years. It wasn't all bad, and we grew up through it—or, at least, I feel I did."

Cadmon and I both nodded.

"You are right," said Cadmon. "We learned a great deal we wouldn't have done otherwise, and we've come home safely. Now we need to rediscover what 'home' means…"

Our reminiscing was interrupted by the sound of horses galloping through the gate into Coningsburh. King Ethelbert and some of the King's Guard drew up a few yards from us. Ethelbert dismounted, handed over the reins and waved his men away.

"Cadmon! I have a task for you!"

"Yes, my Lord?"

"I've been thinking. Our young Thanes could benefit from refreshing their horsemanship skills, not to mention battle tactics. Only the highest standards will do. We haven't had a war for decades now, so training in peacetime has slipped. See what you can do with them, will you."

Without waiting for a reply Ethelbert turned on his heel and strode towards the Royal Hall.

"Well, that's sudden promotion. Think you can manage it?" I teased.

"The question is, can *they* manage it. His men are overweight, undertrained, and ineffective. Whatever I do with them can only be an improvement," Cadmon retorted. "And Tola, you are the Queen's chief person in charge of herbs and remedies!"

I said, " Now, if only someone could appoint me as scribe-in-chief to the royal household, that would make the day for all of us!"

About to enter the Hall, Ethelbert paused and called out. "Alric, whenever I need to meet with the Bishop, I want you to translate for him, and write down a record of our meeting!"

Augustinus was well aware that our mission could come to depend more on Ethelbert's influence among his Earls than all our preaching and teaching put together. This was more than a half-truth. Most people in the Saxon Kingdom were churls—freemen at the bottom of the social ladder, one step above slaves. They followed their overlord in his public religious practices, but adherence alone did not bring health or healing. Through hardship, starvation and disease, their needs were desperate, and few ever reached the age of forty. Among the destitute, some lived in the ruins of the old Roman town in the valley below, others in the dark woods surrounding Coningsburh, and even in the fishing villages around the coast. Augustinus felt the need to minister to anyone, young or old, man or woman, high or lowborn, whose life was marred by diseases of body or mind.

This was his vision, and he would not let it go.

*

Inside the chapel of San Martinus, in preparation for King Ethelbert's baptism, our Roman masons and builders were finishing a six-sided baptismal font, about sixteen inches deep. It was partially sunk into the floor, positioned midway between the west door and chancel steps, five feet in diameter, and built from recovered limestone. Our builder and decorator, Tiberius Centumalus, added the finishing touches of mortar to the lavishly decorated sides. There were benches around the walls, but none in the body of the Chapel itself.

"Nearly done!" Tiberius said, "It'll all be ready for Pentecost. But there's not enough time to extend the Chapel. We'll leave that for a few more weeks then make a start. I think our Bishop will be pleased."

And so he was.

All the while King Ethelbert continued his royal duties of ruling the Kingdom, dealing with dignitaries from neighbouring kingdoms, hosting visitors and coming to the Chapel most days looking for signs of progress. The King's Earls came and went in a steady stream. The thought of a King departing from centuries of Saxon tradition and worship was deeply unsettling to the Saxon overlords of Cantia. They had no taste for abstract, philosophical ideas of a Christian God, while their blood-soaked ancestral gods still held them in thrall. With each one, Ethelbert confided his intention to receive baptism, also stressing that no one was under compulsion to follow in Ethelbert's footsteps.

All the same, something more tangible was needed.

I had yet to discover what that was.

VII
ETHELBERT'S BAPTISM PENTECOST, CHAPEL OF SAN MARTINUS

June, AD 597

IT WAS THE day of King Ethelbert's baptism, and the Chapel at San Martinus was overflowing. All eight of the King's Earls had decided to attend. At the appointed hour we processed with unhurried dignity through the west door, Ethelbert walking barefoot with Augustinus and our monks. Inside the air was thick with the heady scent of incense, and candlelight hazy with perfumed smoke rising from braziers around the walls. The sound of a canticle announced the start of the proceedings, the pure tones of a simple chant adding to the sense of wonder and mystery.

On reaching the font, Augustinus explained the significance of what was about to take place. Ethelbert removed his crown and stepped into the water, kneeling down so that only his head, arms and torso were visible above the waterline. The ritual that followed was markedly different from pagan rituals that slaughtered a bull at the hand of Wodin's High Priest. In the Chapel, no animal was sacrificed, no libation of blood poured out. Instead, Augustinus read from the Gospels, then took a large scallop shell and scooped up blessed water from the baptismal font. Three times Augustinus poured the water over the King's head in the Threefold Name, invisibly making Ethelbert a newborn son and servant of Christ.

Everyone present watched this sacred act intently. Beads of water glistened on Ethelbert's hair like a simple crown, more beautiful even than the one he had briefly surrendered.

Afterwards, the meal that followed in the King's Hall was as boisterous as ever, as Ethelbert's Earls and Thanes toasted their newly baptised King, drinking to Thor as much as to Christ, with no understanding about what the ceremony had meant. An Ode to Ethelbert praised his greatness and fortitude and the new hope that stemmed from the arrival of missionaries from the Pope.

"Syncretism!" Laurentius hissed afterwards between clenched teeth.

"Patience," Augustinus whispered back.

*

Summer wore on. The King and his Court prepared their ships for a fresh round of annual royal visits along the coast of the Kingdom. Coningsburh became a hive of activity, warriors, slaves and servants scurrying back and forth, packing for many weeks away.

Ethelbert and Augustinus met on the last day before the summer round of royal visitations began. I sat with stylus and wax tablet in hand as the King strode back and forth, tugging at his moustache, talking in his usual rapid bursts.

"Bishop, I want to bring my nobles with me in accepting Christ. I am not only their King now - I am their *Christian* King, like the Franks," he glanced at Bertha. "What can I bring them that will persuade my noblemen to follow? If I fail I shall lose my Kingdom, and that would make matters worse for everyone."

I was struck by the King's words. Few attempts had been made over the centuries to win-over hearts and minds among pagan peoples, other than by brute force, whether Greeks or Franks, Africans or Alemanni tribes. Driving our Saxons to water would not make them drink if they had no thirst for the new religion.

"You are right not to force the Christian faith on your people," Augustinus warned the King. "It is a barbaric thing to do, it yields few results and harvests great resentment. No, we haven't come like some fearful tyrant to impose Christ on your Cantwara people."

I had not yet grasped the full implications of a Saxon Warrior-King adopting another religion—how much it affected culture and tradition, the family and the use or abuse of power. Ethelbert, as a semi-religious figure as well as a political leader and warlord, possessed great authority to introduce new customs, religious or otherwise.

"But," Ethelbert cautioned, " I cannot make changes and abandon our ancient beliefs without good reason. Responsibility for my people rests entirely on my shoulders. I am a mediator between my people and their gods at the shrines and temples all over the land— particularly at the shrine of Wodin. They believe that the prosperity of the Kingdom depends on the sacrifices and offerings they make."

Ethelbert strode back and forth as he spoke, greatly agitated.

"Achievements in battle hold the highest honour among us Saxons. Look around you. Young boys are growing into men all over my Kingdom, and they are drawn to those Earls who can give them the best prospects of adventure and plunder—and eventually land, because land is their highest prize of all. But as you can see, our Cantwara people are cut off from easy conquests. We are *far* from the kingdoms that are now emerging on new frontiers to the north and the west. How can our young Thanes learn war if they never see a battle?"

The silence that followed left Ethelbert's question hanging in the air as he continued pacing to and fro.

"There is another possibility," Augustinus suggested. "The ascendency you have won over other Saxon Kingdoms might not be secure forever—unless you achieve victories—but on a different foundation."

He paused for Ethelbert's full attention.

"And that foundation is?"

"Recasting your overlordship role as the supreme peacekeeper and mediator of all the Kingdoms that owe you their fealty. If we were in Rome, I would say that you had the power, or *imperium*, which means very substantial influence."

Somehow, at that moment, a strategy became clear. The bright light of a hundred candles seemed to illuminate Ethelbert's mind.

"Yes! Yes! Now I see the goal I have been searching for! Not to be the solitary Christian Kingdom of Cantia, but a whole Christian nation of tribes and kingdoms! The Church gives us new values, but still leaves place for some of the old. And my overlordship can embrace all these under my patronage. We are in pursuit of Kingdoms!"

Augustinus stood up, the two men walking and talking back and forth, as one idea tumbled out after another.

"Think of King Clovis, the founder of the whole Merovingian dynasty," Augustinus suggested. "As the first Christian King of the Franks nearly a century ago, Clovis established Parisius as his capital city—the same city, of course, that your father-in-law King Charibertus had once ruled," Augustinus bowed respectfully to Bertha. Ethelbert continued, as though Bishop and King were a single mind with two voices.

"And since the time of Clovis, there have been close ties between the Saxons in Cantia and the Franks across the water. My deceased mother and my Queen are both descendants of Clovis. Who else among the Saxon kingdoms can boast that?"

"Indeed, and the Church now holds out to you the possibility of a permanent dynasty that ..."

Without warning, the door flew open and Prince Ethelwald rushed into the room.

"Out!" Ethelbert commanded. "We are in conference! I will speak to you later. Off with you!"

Ethelwald turned to Augustinus, giving him a huge smile as he ran out the door.

As calm returned Augustinus said, "I think you have at least one answer to your earlier question—how you might manage to convince your Earls and Thanes about Christ."

Ethelbert sat down briefly, his hand holding Bertha's.

"How?"

"Your sons will travel with you for the next few months?"

Ethelbert nodded. "Yes, always."

"Your Earls and leading men will wonder what has happened to Ethelwald that he cannot only walk, he can run! You might want to tell them what has happened, and leave your Earls to make up their minds."

Bertha sat up, alarmed. "I don't want my son used as an exhibit for all to see!"

"No, my Queen," Ethelbert smiled. "But if they ask, surely I must give an honest answer."

Augustinus outlined his final thought.

"Perhaps our Roman Church might have a strong claim upon the loyalties of the British Church to the far west of these Isles. From what I learned in Rome before we set out, the British Church grew out of the Roman Church in the old days, as the Province of Britannia. After you Saxons came, the British gradually retreated further and further into the West. They are now allied with the Irish Church. Why not draw them into the influence of Cantia, for the peace and security that you as Overlord can offer them with the Saxons?"

Ethelbert was greatly excited at the prospect.

"Yes, yes, this is perfect! My overlordship already includes a conquered Saxon kingdom, bordering the kingdoms of the Britons. They call themselves the Hwicce. They have a considerable British remnant, but their existence alongside Saxons is unusual—and also intentionally peaceful. Let us make that the place where we begin!"

And yet, for the Queen, for all the brightness from the window, and several burning candles, a shadow seemed to spread across the room.

VIII
THE FIRST FRUITS

July – August, AD 597

I SURVEYED OUR newly completed monastic compound close by Queen Bertha's Chapel of San Martinus. Built by the King's men together with our lay brothers, and Graciosus as joint supervisor, the compound included our hovels, a refectory and kitchen, washing and drying rooms, storage for tools, the Abbot's office, and a room large enough for a small library and teaching.

Augustinus appointed Petrus as the first Abbot, and named the whole compound as the Abbey of San Martinus. Our makeshift Abbey was far from a copy of the San Andreas Monastery in Rome, but it was decidedly our home.

Our daily routine was similar to the pattern of life at San Andreas—praying and singing the monastic offices throughout the day, simple meals, cleaning and washing, the work detail for the day; and for Brother Petrus and me, setting up the library in the hope that students would soon come. Some of our number, under Graciosus's watchful eye, ploughed a nearby field and tended crops to be less-dependant on the generosity of the King.

*

The time had come to take the next steps in our mission. Gathering in the San Martinus Chapel, Augustinus explained a clear and simple strategy.

"The longer we delay our work of mission, the harder it becomes to engage with the churls, the farmers and fishermen around us. I have spoken with King Ethelbert on several occasions now, and he stands firmly with us on this matter. When we first sailed up the Wantsum Channel on our way here to Coningsburh, I noticed many fishing villages along the way. Our task now is to share the story of our faith with these people and to listen to theirs, offering practical help, such as Tola's ointments and remedies, or farming expertise—and praying for whatever spiritual or physical needs the people may have. Be ready to bless or simply to be present, even at sacrificial feasts during the seasons of the year. Later, we may be able to go a step further, and encourage the folk working the land and the water to remove idols from hilltop sanctuaries, shrines and sacred precincts, but keep those places for worship by the placing of a cross. We must adapt as we proceed, as I know the Pope would certainly do. Perhaps half a dozen groups, each comprising, say three or four people—a monk, a priest, and a lay brother perhaps where their skills might be useful. We begin tomorrow morning."

Prior Laurentius tackled Augustinus immediately on leaving the Chapel. I followed close enough to hear the heated exchange that followed. Laurentius was the most aloof and distant member of our company, often expressing his anger to Augustinus when the two of them were alone. Now all Laurentius's patrician instincts came rushing to the fore.

"Are you deranged, Bishop?" he spat out. "This is not what the Pope would have wanted!"

Augustinus suppressed his irritation.

"And what do you believe the Pope would have wanted, Laurentius?"

Laurentius was a firm believer that it was a duty to exert his will, and said, "His Holiness would *enforce* adherence to the Christian faith through the King."

Augustinus responded patiently, "I suggest you raise this with the King, but what you propose is *exactly* what he and I have both rejected. Did we come to Cantia with an army? No! The King knows his people must come willingly, and not by fear or compulsion. Ethelbert has left now to visit different parts of the Kingdom. He should be back before winter sets in, and you can raise this issue with him when he returns. Meanwhile, Laurentius, we will begin in the manner that the King and I have already agreed."

*

So began the next stage of our mission. Augustinus, Wulfrun, Tola and I journeyed on foot to Fordwic and took a boat further downstream. Arriving at the first settlement, we anchored our boat and stepped ashore. Tola pointed to several tall, ancient weeping willows in full leaf, their enormous gnarled roots sinking deep into the water.

"It's not only herbs we use for medicine, Alric," she pointed out. "That bark's also good for colds and fevers and reducing swollen joints." She stooped down and picked up a twig. "Here! Next time you have a pain Alric, chew this."

I nodded and absently stuck the twig into my pocket, my thoughts elsewhere as we came in sight of some fishing boats tied up alongside the grassy bank. The village bustled with activity, dogs barked at our arrival, chickens scratching in the compound and pigs jostling and grunting at the trough. Some members of the village were busy with children, others spinning strands of wool or gathering up firewood, while older members sat weaving and chatting in the sunshine outside their hovels.

The clothing we wore was much the same as everyone's— woollen, dull and simple. Fishermen unloading a catch looked up as we approached, curious rather than hostile, and returned our greeting. A young woman, Tola's age perhaps, came down to the river to fetch some of the baskets of fish.

"Here, let me help you", said Tola. "My brother Alric and I have come back after seven years away from Sandwic Haven. It's good to be home again!"

The young woman stared in surprise. "Don't I know you?" she exclaimed. "You and your brother were taken away somewhere by some horrible men, nobody really knows where. We used to play with you at the Fair at Ratteburg, remember? *Everybody* knows your story! For years we've been asking your mother for news, but she's always had none. Come, let's get this fish up to the shed, and you can tell us everything!"

As we entered the village, the young woman called out, "Ma, look! This is Tola! The one who was stolen from her mother!"

We could scarcely have expected a warmer welcome.

After Tola had finished telling her story and answered many questions, everyone fell quiet, mulling over what she had said. To break the silence, she asked "Is there anyone here who is ill or suffering at the moment? I have brought some herbs and potions with me that might help."

There were several needs, ranging from stomach problems and dry coughs to painful joints and infected wounds that would not heal. Tola went around to each one, using the potions and ointments where she could.

Later, with all the fish unloaded, the men and young lads of the village joined us to hear what we had to say. I told them that King Ethelbert himself had invited us into his Kingdom, and explained why we had come to visit them.

Augustinus sat on his low milking stool without his mitre, making himself less imposing, as San Martinus had done centuries earlier in the hamlets around Turones, and added, "This is a fishing village Alric, and you were once a fisherman? Tell us about the Norse god Neorth and your shrine at home."

I spoke of Neorth, the god of the sea, and how I had never left home on the waters without paying a small tribute to him, as most fishermen did, and told of how distant and feckless he had proved to be on the day that we—Cadmon, Tola and I—needed him most when we were seized from our home by slavers.

I said, "On that morning, Wyrd and her sisters sat in the clouds, weaving the tapestry of my life. They stopped suddenly, leaving me dangling by a thread, and I greatly feared that I might be cast off into some outer darkness. But an invisible hand seemed to grasp my thread and hold it fast, sparing my life. From that moment, the thread has been held in the hand of God I now serve, the bringer of life. And so, after five months at sea, I came to Rome and was cared for by followers of the One God, under whose protection I now live. Through all our troubles, he brought us home again! My brethren, may I say this: you, whose lives are spent labouring on the water, you too may want to think with great care about whose protection you are asking for, when you next climb into your boat!"

We said our farewells and returned to our boat, escorted by half the village.

As we pushed away from the riverbank, Augustinus asked,

"Alric, do we have time to visit your family at the Haven before dusk?"

*

At the quay, Godric was finishing his labours for the day. Seeing Tola he glanced up, and I waved. He stared a moment, recognised who we were, and turned back to his task. Mama gave Tola a big hug as we arrived. I introduced Bishop Augustinus and Wulfrun to Pa and Ma and Greta, and everyone else as we walked over to a blazing outdoor fire nearby the hamlet's small communal hall.

Augustinus said, "It seemed a good idea, as we were so nearby, to come and meet you at last! Alric lived in our monastery in Rome for several years, as you know already; and Wulfrun joined us on our way through the Kingdoms of Francia to help us in our mission."

Mama was a little in awe of Augustinus, tall in his brown habit, but she was charmed by his warm smile. As the bread was shared, soup ladled and the beer flowed, conversation switched to our impressions of the Kingdom, and particularly Coningsburh, the King's fortress on the hill, and the mournfully deserted Roman city below.

"Inside those walls, dogs howl in the dark!" I teased Greta, snuggling-up against my arm. "And the wolves come sniffing for little girls like you!"

Greta screeched, "Don't! That's horrible! I don't like wolves!"

"Not even tame ones?"

"There aren't any tame ones!" she snorted at my ignorance.

Augustinus watched, smiling as we bantered back and forth together. Wulfrun struck up a conversation with Godric, but he was guarded and showed little interest. The evening wore on, and it was a long time before we found our way to a bed.

Once again, only Godric seemed unmoved by our arrival.

*

The following morning I left Augustinus and Wulfrun talking with Pa, while I accompanied Tola to inspect the layout of her herb garden near the rear gate that led into the forest. A low fence surrounded the pots and plants in an area of ten-by-ten paces, keeping out the chickens that otherwise had free run of our whole enclosure.

"What are you hoping to achieve, Tola?"

"You know I can't bear barren soil. I love things that grow, Alric—flowers and food, but especially herbs. Healing those who are ill is what draws me the most."

"I believe you. Tell me what you've planted in here."

Tola swiftly ran an eye over her growing collection. "You see, everything's in earthenware pots? That's so I can choose the right soil to go with each herb—and it also keeps the caterpillars out. I think you know already that every person is said to have four 'humours' that help the body to balance its wellbeing?" I shook my head.

"Well, physicians speak of these as four elements—blood for air, phlegm for water, yellow bile for fire, and black bile for the earth. These humours wax and wane in the body, depending on what we eat, and what activities we do. The herbs help to restore our balance when we fall ill. As you can see, I have nine different herbs planted in these pots."

Tola pointed to each pot in turn as we walked our way around her garden.

"This pot has sage. It cleanses the body of venom and pestilence. Now in this pot, I've planted betony. It can cure almost anything—chills, upset blood, and even fear."

"Powerful indeed," I exclaimed." I now understand why you are so fearless."

"Also, there's clary sage. You should know this, Alric. It's also called 'Oculus Christi', the Eye of Christ?"

"Used for?"

"Eyewash, you idiot! I thought you were the Latin scholar!"

We circled most of the herb garden. Tola continued, "Now, the next one here is hyssop—taken as a hot drink in oil, wine or syrup, it warms away cold catarrhs and chest phlegm."

"And this one?"

"This is camomile. The flowers are good for making infusions for digestion, and sedative mixtures. You'll also be glad to learn, Alric, that they can also do something about that flatulence of yours as well! And as a bonus, it's also a remedy against poison—for when you get on your companions' nerves!"

"I should have learned all of this years ago, Tola! What a marvellous specimen I would be today!"

"No, I think some people are simply incurable!"

We walked around a little further.

"And there's comfrey—useful for healing wounds and inflammations—and it helps broken bones to set too…"

A thunder of hooves coming from the forest interrupted us, stopping at the gate. I recognised the messenger as he reined in his horse and demanded, "Is the Bishop here?"

Pa had also noticed the arrival and strode quickly towards us.

"Here is the Bishop," he gestured. "Who asks, and what is it you want of him?"

"I am the King's Messenger, I come at his orders. He is nearby at Eastringe, on his first visitation this season. Bishop, you are to come at once—and bring Alric, the one who speaks our tongue. I have brought two horses. I see there are three of you. One of you will have to walk."

"Here," Pa said to Wulfrun, "take my horse."

We galloped beneath the boughs of giant oaks and elms, sunlight barely filtering through this tightly knit canopy. Well within the hour we dismounted at Ethelbert's Mead Hall at Eastringe and followed the messenger into the cool, half-light of a somewhat gloomy reception room.

We sat and waited for nearly an hour until finally the door was thrown open and Ethelbert burst in.

Without a greeting or preamble, he came straight to the point.

"You remember Coifin? The High Priest who attended dinner when you arrived?"

We nodded.

"He is the caretaker of Wodin's shrine, a mile from here. He has come to my Hall for a meeting with Earl Sighart and others. He wants no dealings with Christ, however softly I approach him. Coifin has brought a woman steeped in witchcraft to contend with you, Bishop, and unmask you as a fraud. He wants a contest with you tonight. Are you willing?"

We looked anxiously at Augustinus. He smiled and said, "Of course. From the earliest days, the Church has set its face against witchcraft. It is evil, and it is manipulative. What I know of pagan priests is that they practise magic using spells to bind others, or divinations claiming to know where things are that were lost, and offering love-magic from amulets, or as lucky charms, and they use potions to trick others to do their will. And their rituals make no sense. Whatever god they make offerings to, all these are nothing more than wood, stone or precious metals. They have no ultimate power."

"Well, that all sounds reassuring," Ethelbert responded, relaxing a little.

"But also, you must understand that I have no special powers within myself," Augustinus added. "I have nothing except what God gives to me at the moment of need. I can't plan ahead; I can only be open to hearing Christ's command, and wait. I am no more than a servant of the Lord who commands 'Come here!' or, 'Go there!'"

Ethelbert mused, "I have not known servanthood since I became King."

Augustinus looked at Ethelbert.

"And I have only known freedom since I became a slave of Christ."

*

By late afternoon, the Hall was full of people from the hamlet and farms in the area, waiting for a glimpse of their King. The Steward seated Augustinus beside the King, with Earl Sighart and Cadmon's brother Derian to his left. Wulfrun and I sat together, noting each new arrival as they entered the Hall. After Ethelbert's words of welcome and a glowing introduction for Augustinus, the food was served.

Halfway through the meal, without announcement or introduction, a woman dramatically appeared in the doorway of the King's Hall, dressed in dark garments and framed against the dwindling rays of the evening sun.

"Ah, the witch!" murmured the lips of some, as she stepped boldly into the centre of the Hall as though it was her own. She spun around and around on her heel, making a circle, her wand-stick outstretched and pointing, thrusting, as though searching out someone. A tense silence fell, and the taste of fear became suddenly palpable. Abruptly, the woman stopped, her stick pointing at one of the serving maids as she weaved her way around the tables with a tray of food. No one else moved. In the unnerving silence, the young woman turned, looking back over her shoulder, and dropped her tray in fright.

"Come here, you fool!" the witch commanded, swishing the layers of black fabric of her dress back and forth, her dark veil pulled down over face and long, straggly hair. "Kneel before me!" she cried in a loud, dominating voice. Everyone leaned forward, enthralled to see how matters would now unfold.

Earl Sighart whispered to Augustinus, "Her name is Evanora—a witch, in league with Coifin. She has her coven there."

"What is it that you wish for, woman?" the witch demanded in a voice as loud as the crack of doom. The serving maid's reply was too soft for us to hear, but Evanora repeated her words out loud.

"You have lost your lover, you say; and you want him back again, do you?"

The witch began her spell-making with incomprehensible words, circling the poor girl with steps that mimicked the movement of a long-legged spider, all the while waving a cloud of perfume around the serving maid's head, and flicking liquid at her from a leafy stick in her hand.

As Evanora's loud incantations continued, I began to hear a softer sound close by. Beginning as a chortle, the sound slowly grew louder, becoming a low belly laugh before turning into a full-blown roar of uninhibited mirth.

By now our Bishop was on his feet, caught up in a laughter that stemmed from a deep feeling of inward joy, filling the Hall, changing the atmosphere. The effect was contagious. Wulfrun and I stood to join Augustinus; then others, and yet more until the Hall was in an uproar of laughter. The witch stopped her spell weaving and looked around angrily at the sea of faces laughing and banging on the tables. She turned, and fled out the door and into the dark.

When the laughter eventually subsided and eyes wiped dry, the King turned to Coifin.

"And you had the temerity to bring this witch into my Hall?" he accused, shaking his head slowly in deep disappointment. This time, Coifin slunk away without a word. Ethelbert spoke into the silence that followed.

"Tonight," he began with great gravitas, "we have been witness to a changing world. Coifin claims to be the High Priest of Wodin. So be it; that is what he wishes to believe. But know this; Wodin is a name I accept as my founding ancestor, but not the name of my God!"

Ethelbert went on to tell the story of the healing of his younger son, and his decision to follow Christ by whom such a miracle had taken place.

"For most of us, I know, it is no simple thing to turn aside from the gods whom we have served for generations, and I make no demands on you to do so, until your moment comes. For all of our sakes, my wish is that it will be soon!"

*

Summer turned into autumn, and late autumn into winter. The King returned from his visitations and requested all his Earls and Thanes to receive baptism.

In the last days of December, great numbers of noblemen and warriors arrived at Rofesburh, at the crossing of the River Medd-Way. Early in the morning Ethelbert and Augustinus stood on the slope of a low hill above the broad river, observing the long sweeping curve of water as it flowed slowly northwards into the Temes Estuary. Below us, Waeclinga Straet stretched from Ratteburg Fort on the east coast to Lundenwic in the west, and nearby the road crossed over an ancient Roman bridge. The slope of the hill provided a natural amphitheatre, large enough to seat a thousand people spread out on the grassy riverbank.

Despite Ethelbert's energetic support, the success of our mission was by no means guaranteed. For the first time since our arrival at Easter, the King now stood to lose as much as Augustinus. Most of those who came on that day worked the land or fished the rivers and coastline, but there was also an elite group of aristocratic warriors led by seven of the Earls. A warrior was highly unlikely to convert if his chief did not.

The rains held off, and the weather turned unseasonably mild for winter. The Earls and their men talked and joked together, gathered around their standards. Our companions from the Abbey of San Martinus stood near the water's edge. At noon, Ethelbert addressed his subjects, welcoming everyone, and explaining why they had gathered together. Augustinus came forward with staff in hand and a mitre on his head. A little shakily, I rose to my feet and stood at his side to translate.

When he had finished speaking, Augustinus stepped into the cold water and looked back. "Laurentius! Wulfrun! All our Priests! Follow me, there are many coming down!" With obvious reluctance, Laurentius entered the water, his teeth chattering, deeply sceptical that this approach to winning-over Saxon hearts and minds would ever work.

"Voluntary conversions don't last!" was his consistent declaration. "Everyone becomes hysterical for a while, it wears off, and in the end, there is no change in religious practices. Anything except brute force and compulsion is a waste of time!"

Augustinus smiled reassuringly as Sighart, the eighth Earl, took his first step into the river and stood with head bowed. This was the baptism the Bishop had promised him. Augustinus scooped up water with his scallop and carefully poured it over Sighart's head, pronouncing the Threefold Name of Father, Son and Holy Spirit, then marked the sign of the cross on the Earl's forehead. Sighart returned to the bank and stood by as each of his Thanes and warriors from Ratteburg came forward and entered the water.

*

That night in his Mead Hall the Earl of Rofesburh drank deep from his goblet, then as he pulled a piece of pork from his knife with his fingers, he turned to Cadmon.

"So, young man, what lies ahead for you?" The pork vanished into the Earl's mouth, his thick grey beard moving back and forth as he chewed the meat, his eyes rheumy beneath thick eyebrows and unkempt grey hair. I could not recall whether he had entered the water. Perhaps he believed being host to the King was sufficient recompense without the need to add a baptism.

Cadmon spoke of his time in the Roman cavalry and observed, "I'm not clear how Saxon horses are deployed in battle, as our warriors haven't been at war for decades. The horses here are small, compared to war-horses in Rome, and no one receives battle training, so far as I can ascertain. Our horses here in Cantia are mostly used for scouting—or transport, using their horses to get them to the battlefront. Then they dismount and fight on foot alongside the warriors in a shield wall. The King realises that the *fyrd* needs a riding school and thorough training in using their weapons on horseback. Otherwise, there's hardly any point in having cavalry."

The Earl laughed dismissively.

"Well, we won't be sending you any of *my* warriors, young man! Our men ride horses from birth! No, no, we do not need to train men for something they are already born to do! I think you will find your school to be a waste of time!"

Cadmon responded, "Well, the King has instructed that I open a Cavalry School for young Thanes so they can learn the rudiments of horsemanship, combat and so forth."

"How extraordinary!" the Earl responded as he sliced another piece of pork.

Cadmon smiled a smile that said, 'Your day will come!'

IX
CATHEDRAL

January, AD 598

BISHOP AUGUSTINUS PUT his head around the open doorway into the Scriptorium.

"Come Alric! We have been summoned!"

We hastened from the Abbey up the steep path to Coningsburh and into the royal apartments. True to his manner, Ethelbert came straight to the point.

"After what took place at the Medd-Way, Bishop, the time is now ripe for us to look ahead and see further than perhaps we could before."

Ethelbert turned to Bertha.

"I understand it is customary in Francia and Rome and Constantinople for a Bishop to have a Cathedral. Is that not so, my Queen?"

Bertha nodded. "That is so, my Lord. Civilized countries all follow that practice."

The Roman method was to build a cathedral, grand buildings and open squares, markets, piped water, baths, civic statues and lavish townhouses, all within the city walls.

"My Queen and I have been considering this matter. Now is the time to begin building your Cathedral, Bishop! As your King, the expense will fall to me."

Augustinus was stunned. Finding his voice, he responded,

"That is most generous, King Ethelbert!"

Ethelbert quickly added, as he looked at Bertha, "And the Cathedral should be close enough for you to walk to whenever you want, my Queen."

He turned to Augustinus.

"But there is also another matter, Bishop. Perhaps you should explain." Ethelbert turned to his Queen.

Bertha paused, thinking how best to express her request.

"This is what is on my mind, Bishop," she began. "You know that my Father, King Charibertus, was refused burial in Parisius, which was his own city. His preference would have been to be buried at the Abbey of San Denys. But after his death he was excommunicated from the Church, and buried far from Parisius—on the coast called Tractatus Armoricani, within the fortress of Blavia Castellum."

Bertha hesitated to speak of what weighed on her mind. She said, "I believe that you know my father had four wives. His outrageous behaviour was a stain on the Church—but despite that, he was still my father. It troubles me that he was denied burial on holy ground. So, our request to you, Bishop, is that we build a monastery with a chapel that includes a mausoleum so that when our time on earth is over, we may be buried on consecrated ground. Our descendants, too, will have a place there, as will you, Bishop Augustinus, and all future bishops of the Cathedral."

Now it was Augustinus's turn to reflect on what Bertha had said.

"A dynastic mausoleum within a monastic chapel," he mused.

"This will also be our gift to the Church, of course," Ethelbert hurried to assure Augustinus. "And you can open a school in the monastery too," looking pointedly at me, "so that what you promised us about education when we first met at Ratteburg fort, will now come to fruition."

Augustinus nodded in agreement.

"This is an inspired idea, and a most generous gift! May I suggest that, as we already have a temporary Abbey, we build the Cathedral first, as a clear sign that we mean to remain here, and then afterwards build the monastery outside the city walls as soon as resources allow."

"Excellent!" said Ethelbert. "We are still young. We can wait—a little while!"

We left the royal apartments and climbed the parapet, looking out over the forlorn shell of a city in the valley below, and tried to imagine places where the Cathedral might be built.

Ethelbert surveyed the ancient Roman road circling around the crumbling walls and broken gates. "We will repair the walls and the gates, and I will build a new gate, The Queen's Gate, just for you, my Queen."

"I like that!" she laughed.

There was little else to laugh about. The task was enormous. Barely visible beneath the rubble were two streets that once led towards Eastringe and Fordwic. We could not tell what had once stood there in days long gone, but between these two roads was a large piece of ground that Ethelbert now earmarked for the building of the Cathedral.

"What will you call it?" Bertha asked.

Augustinus said, "Let us dedicate the Cathedral *Christus Jesus, Sancti Salvatoris* - Jesus Christ, the Holy Saviour!"

Bertha laughed. "Excellent, Bishop, excellent choice!"

"And where would be a good place for the monastery?" Ethelbert asked.

Augustinus examined the area between Coningsburh and the old city wall, about half a mile away. "Perhaps down there on open ground, between the Chapel of San Martinus and the intended site of the Cathedral. There's sufficient land to grow crops there for the monastery too."

"And you have a name for its dedication?" Bertha pressed the Bishop.

"Ah, I think that will have to be the two most significant apostles in —*Sanctorum Petri et Pauli*—St Peter and St Paul."

Augustinus turned to Ethelbert in genuine admiration.

"You are giving us two magnificent gifts. Words cannot express our gratitude for your great generosity!"

"I see this as my *duty*, Bishop. May the work proceed with all speed," and the two men clasped hands in friendship, in the Roman manner.

"Are you going to rename the old town?" Augustinus asked the King. "The Romans called it Durovernum Cantiacorum."

Ethelbert shook his head. "We have always called it Cantwaraburh - the city of the Cantwara people."

Augustinus nodded, and took the opportunity to share something that was uppermost in his mind.

"Whether we baptised a thousand or ten thousand at the Medd-Way, I cannot say. But what is clear to me is that we now need reinforcements for the mission. I propose to send two of my monks back to Rome, and request that Pope Gregorius send more missionaries to assist us."

"Excellent, Bishop! You have made a good beginning—don't lose the initiative! I leave it in your hands."

As the Bishop and I walked the short distance to our Abbey, my thoughts drifted painfully back to Rome, and the precarious position of the Holy City. Paulina was there too, sharing in that daily uncertainty. Merely one day would be enough for the Germanic tribe of Langobards to break down the gates and enter the city, plundering and burning until not one soul was left alive.

Yet here we were now, planning to bring an ancient Roman town back from the dead.

X
RETURN TO ROME
AD 598

WITH THE ARRIVAL of spring, Augustinus commissioned Abbot Petrus and Prior Laurentius to prepare for a return to Rome. This was after Eostre, when the weather might be favourable for a sea crossing to Quentovicus. They were to be accompanied by Cadmon and four warriors from his Cavalry School for support and protection on their journey.

On the eve of departure, Tola and I travelled to Ratteburg to bid Cadmon farewell. There was none of our usual banter over the evening meal, all of us only too aware of the dangers on the journey ahead. Cadmon outlined their planned route for Sighart and Odelinda.

"We'll make our way south from Quentovicus to Parisius, and aim to bypass Cabillonum."

"To avoid Brunhild and Count Warnachar?" I queried.

"Yes, if possible. And no doubt on our return we'll be loaded with letters to deliver for the Pope."

"And the books for our library!" I was excited by the prospect.

"I thought you weren't going on these long trips again," Tola broke in quietly, her face taught and lips pursed. Cadmon also seemed a little uneasy. Odelinda looked up sharply at her son, but said nothing.

Cadmon said, "Well, I had no plans to travel at all, but the Bishop has commissioned me, the King has agreed, and here I am, ready to leave."

The following morning, standing on the quayside below Ratteburg fort, we hardly spoke a word. Tola wiped her eyes as the ship pulled away, and we waved goodbye until the ship left the estuary and slipped out of sight towards the southeast.

"So tearful, my sister?" I whispered, "I thought you couldn't stand him. You argue most of the time when you're together."

For once, Tola made no reply.

*

Taking our leave of Odelinda and Sighart, Tola and I returned to the Haven. Tola, in a sombre mood, headed straight for her herb garden and I followed her, watching as she spent some time tending her herbs. The spring sun was gaining strength, and in the middle of the day, we decided to walk into the woods beyond our hamlet to take advantage of the dappled shade. With basket in hand, Tola led the way, her eyes searching for herbs and plants to add to her collection.

We took the path towards Eastringe, the woods alive with birdsong. In the distance the dull sound of horse-hoofs carried on the still air. The hoof beats grew louder until ahead of us four riders entered the clearing. I recognised Derian at once. He drew up, the horse sweating under Derian's great weight.

"Whoa!" he cried out, pulling in the reins, "Who do we have here?"

Charm is one thing, lust is quite another. Tola gave only a brief curtsy.

"I am Tola, and this is my brother. Alric."

Derian gave me a sour look.

'Yes, I know who *he* is, Cadmon's friend. Such poor taste."

Derian turned to Tola. "And what are you doing out here in the forest, my dear?" he leered.

Tola made no reply.

Derian continued, "I have heard that my brother is returning to Rome. When might he be expected to return?"

"Ask your father. He may be better placed to answer your question," Tola retorted, stung by the reminder of Cadmon's absence.

Derian's face grew dark with anger.

"So, she has a sharp tongue, does she not?" Derian said, half-turning to his riders. "You deserve a lesson in manners, woman! I'll take you back to Eastringe to teach you some!"

Tola dropped her basket and took a step backwards. "Don't you come near me!" she shouted, moving back another step or two. Derian urged his horse forward and reached down, grabbing at Tola's arm in an effort to drag her onto his horse, but she pulled herself free.

"Crafty little cow!" Derian spat, his anger rising at losing face in front of his companions. "Come here!"

Tola stepped back again, instinctively raising her hands, and screamed. The horse reared up and neighed in fright, throwing Derian off its back.

I grabbed Tola's hand, and in the confusion behind us we raced back to the gate. I shut and bolted it from the inside while Tola ran crying down to our family hovel.

Derian yelled out behind the gate, "You'll pay for this, you little bitch! All of you!"

The shouts and the sound of horses gradually receded as the men rode away back to Eastringe.

Pa, who had been thatching a roof nearby, heard the noise and shouts and climbed down the ladder as Mama rushed out from the weaving shed.

"What is it? What's happened?" she demanded, putting a protective arm around Tola's shoulder.

Between us, the story tumbled out.

Pa was nearly purple with anger.

"We can't leave it like this! Tola, you stay here. Alric, you come with me!"

Pa was seldom angry, but when he was, no one dared stand in his way.

We marched down to the quay.

"We're going to Ratteburg!" he called out to Godric. "Keep cutting the reeds for the roof. We'll be back in a while."

Pa and I rowed strongly with the incoming tide and soon came to the landing-place at Ratteburg, secured the boat, and made our way up to the manor. Sighart was surprised to see us, but gave us a cordial greeting as always.

"Well, Galen, how can I help you?"

"I regret to bring this matter to you, my Lord," Pa began, feeling extremely uncomfortable, "but we come to you as our local magistrate to bring a case for your judgment."

A cloud passed over Sighart's face, his forehead furrowing as he listened.

"Earlier today, Tola and Alric were in the woods behind the Haven, picking herbs for Tola's medications. Four men on horseback accosted them, and one attempted to take Tola away by force."

At that moment I realised how serious this allegation was, and how damaging the outcome could have been for Tola's future.

"Tola fought back and managed to run to the safety of our compound," I began.

My father was visibly shaking as I finished our story. Sighart shook his head in displeasure, his anger growing as he listened.

"Galen, what is your request?"

"It's not compensation that I seek on behalf of my daughter, my Lord. It's justice."

Sighart nodded. "You have spoken well. But do you know who this villain is? Or where he hails from?"

Pa looked at me. "Alric was there as a witness."

My mouth was dry. I cleared my throat.

"It was Derian—your son, Derian."

Sighart's face expressed his shock.

"My son!"

"I'm afraid so, my Lord. Tola will also testify to that, and Derian's three companions also witnessed everything that took place."

Sighart was silent, gazing out to sea. He turned to one of his men.

"I want four horsemen, all armed. And my horse—and horses for Galen and Alric too."

Without a word, Sighart led the way to his Eastringe estate, taking the ancient Roman road from Ratteburg fort towards Coningsburh, then branching off for a few miles in the direction of the Port of Dubras. We rode close by Wodin's shrine on a hilltop overlooking the distant sea, and after a mile or so entered the outskirts of the hamlet.

Arriving at the Eastringe Mead Hall I glanced about the yard, not particularly well kept. The horses I had seen earlier in the woods near the Haven stood tethered outside the stables. A stable hand was dispatched to find Derian. He came out, startled to see us, bowing obsequiously, making a great show of welcoming Sighart, his eyes fixing on Pa and me.

"How say you to this charge?" Sighart snapped. "That this morning, at the Haven, you did assault and attempt to abduct the young woman Tola, daughter of Galen and Erlina, and sister of Alric, who was witness to these events?"

I expected Derian would attempt to deny it all or shift the blame to me, but he wasn't quick-witted enough.

"We had some light-hearted banter, Father, nothing at all to warrant such a prestigious gathering as this!" he gestured with a sweep of his hand.

The Earl stared at his son with contempt. At last, the scales had fallen from Sighart's eyes, and he was willing to see what manner of a man stood before him. And what he saw, he despised.

"Where are your three companions of this morning?" Sighart demanded.

They stepped from the shadows from where they had been nervously watching.

Reluctantly, they walked across the yard and stood before Sighart.

"Alric, tell them what you told me!"

Sighart did not take his eyes off the three witnesses while I spoke, his eyes boring into each man's soul.

Afterwards Earl Sighart demanded, "Do you corroborate what Derian has said of his actions this morning, or do you deny them, and support what Alric has claimed?"

Damned if I do, and damned if I don't, crossed my mind.

"Well? What say you?" Sighart demanded.

They nodded. "It is as the witness has said, my Lord."

Sighart dismounted and confronted Derian.

"Tie his hands wide apart to the stable door, and the same with his feet."

The Earl took a whip from his saddle.

"No, Pa!" Derian begged, but his pleas fell on deaf ears.

I grew wiser that day.

I came to grasp the difference between Law and Justice. The Law would have exacted a price of silver pieces, given to my father. But what was that to the son of a wealthy Earl? No, justice demanded something much harder, and much more painful, than a few pieces of silver.

Odelinda arrived from Ratteburg early the next day to see Mama.

"Erlina, I am so sorry! What can I say? I had no idea Derian has turned into such a self-serving monster!" They fell into each other's arms and cried as only parents can at a moment such as this. Tola came down from her herb garden and Odelinda hugged her close, begging forgiveness, and the two wept together.

"He was always a difficult child," Odelinda recalled, brushing away a tear. "Clinging and dependent. He sometimes bullied Cadmon when he didn't think I was looking. But now he runs one of the estates with his hired men, and he's turned into a monster! He bullies his way through life. I realise now that he always has."

Odelinda reassured Tola, "He won't come near you again, I promise you—Sighart has forbidden him."

I thought, no matter how long it takes, Derian won't forget. He will find another way to get his own back—on all of us.

*

On the brow of the King's hill that is Coningsburh, Tola and Brother John continued to work on Queen Bertha's herb garden, planting and growing herbs to make medicines, ointments and balms. Augustinus resumed his mission to fishing villages around the Wantsum, and between these excursions I began tutoring a small class of three young boys, the first to study in our monastic community.

The King and Augustinus shared my concern for education, and I imagined that Abbot Petrus at that moment might be selecting books and manuscripts from Agapito's Library in Rome for our own Abbey in Cantia.

The months passed by, and summer gave way to a golden autumn. Yet there was still no news of Cadmon, Laurentius—or Petrus.

XI
GREGORIAN LETTERS
Winter, AD 598

THE DAYS HAD shortened into winter long before Cadmon, Petrus and Laurentius returned from Rome, sparking much excitement at the Abbey as we were reunited with our companions. Laurentius, particularly, seemed invigorated by his travels, and supplied a mine of gossip over recent events in the Holy City.

"We have a new Abbot at San Andreas," he said approvingly.

"And who might the 'we' be?" Augustinus interposed, a little irritated by Laurentius's self-serving familiarity.

"Mellitus," Laurentius said. "A true Roman with an aristocratic background, well-educated and suited for the role. We lodged at the monastery while we were in Rome, so we saw quite a bit of him."

"And what of Rome?" Augustinus prodded.

"Rome finds herself in a slightly better place than when we left the city. The Exarch Romanus, a thorn in the Pope's side these last eight years, was finally laid to rest. His successor, Gallinicus, has concluded an armistice between Emperor Mauricius and the Langobards, by accepting their right as rulers of the lands they already occupy. This relieves Rome of another crippling payment to King Agilulf, and the Holy City is beginning to return to some semblance of normality."

"So," Augustinus queried, "does His Holiness now put less emphasis on the End Times than he was accustomed to doing? After all, that was the impetus behind launching this mission."

Laurentius paused.

"His Holiness still holds to the belief that the End Times are imminent, but perhaps we have more breathing space than he had originally anticipated. That Pale Horseman of the plague, that Angel of Death, has not put in another appearance in Rome since we left."

"And you, Petrus?" Augustinus raised an eyebrow.

"We return with a lifetime of books!" Petrus said. "It turned out to be a far easier journey than our first."

He looked paler than usual, somewhat tired after the long journey.

Laurentius broke in, "I have also brought back with me Pope Gregorius's responses to your questions about the running of the Cathedral, Bishop. His document is called the *Libellus Responsionum*, how to organise our clergy. I'm sure you will find this of great interest."

"And what have you to share with us of the journey, Cadmon? Did everything proceed smoothly?"

"Much easier than our previous journey here, as Brother Petrus has said. We followed much the route as we had done before, but this time without going to Turones or Aurelianorum, avoiding another encounter with both Queen Brunhild and King Chlothar."

Laurentius handed Augustinus a document along with a bundle of letters; but with my students waiting, I did not loiter to discover to whom they were written, or what their contents might be.

After supper Cadmon and I approached Augustinus with a request.

"Bishop, if you have no immediate need for Cadmon's services or mine, I wondered if we may have a few days with our families over this season? Tola has already returned to the Haven, and Cadmon's riders to Ratteburg."

With Augustinus's blessing, we set off on the morrow from Fordwic. I had expected that Cadmon would want to disembark at Ratteburg, but he had another idea.

"I'll come with you directly to the Haven," he decided.

A few hours later, we entered by the gate on the quay. Pa and

Godric stood talking outside one of their favourite places, beneath the eaves of the haddock smoking-shed. We joined them there, exchanging greetings.

Cadmon's eye was fixed on Pa. He came straight to the point.

"Sir, I have come to ask for your daughter Tola's hand in marriage."

My jaw dropped; Cadmon had mentioned none of his plans to me on our journey down to the Haven.

Pa hesitated for a moment.

"Have you asked Tola, Cadmon? She must speak for herself."

Cadmon glanced around.

"Where is she?"

"In our hovel," Pa gestured down the grassy slope.

Cadmon turned on his heel and strode purposefully to the hovel door. All eyes followed him as he tapped on the doorpost. Peering into the gloom, he bent low and disappeared inside.

Pa and I looked at each other with raised eyebrows. Mama and Greta, on hearing Cadmon's voice, had come out from the weaving shed and joined us where we stood. Galen told them what was happening, and I expected to see the happy couple emerging at any moment, hand in hand, coming to greet us with their good news.

Instead, the sound of Tola's voice cut through the air, with Cadmon's deeper tone replying. Tola's voice grew louder, and in a moment both were shouting. A first-class row was in progress, their angry shouts carrying across the compound. Mama's sister Helga appeared with my uncle, and joined us under the eaves.

"Cadmon's proposing to Tola," Pa explained.

Our small crowd of onlookers began to swell.

Mama's hand covered her mouth, her eyes fixed on their hovel door, expecting the worst as the shouts increased in volume. She glanced at Pa. He shrugged and shook his head.

With a final shout from Tola, Cadmon emerged from the hovel, his jaw set.

It's all over, I thought, she's thrown it away. I always knew her sarcastic temper would do her no good.

All eyes were fixed on Cadmon as he strode back to us.

Pa raised a quizzical eyebrow, shaking his head in anticipation of Cadmon's answer.

Cadmon came to a standstill, his breathing become calmer.

A hush fell. Even the woods seemed to go silent.

Cadmon looked up, and drew a deep breath.

"She said yes!"

Pa let out a huge sigh of relief.

"Then you may wed my daughter," he declared, grasping Cadmon's hand while Mama and Helga ran full speed to our hovel, shrieking in delight. Tola came out a short while later, arm in arm with Mama and Helga, now serene and composed, as though nothing untoward had ever happened, ready to receive the congratulations of our family, and the blessing of the whole community.

"Well, that's a good start!" Pa said with irony, and we escorted the groom down the grassy slope to meet his intended and congratulate his future mother-in-law.

Later that day, I rowed Cadmon to Ratteburg. After several minutes when neither of us spoke I finally asked, "You've been thinking about this for a while?"

Cadmon came back from his private thoughts.

"Yes, Alric, I have. During that first long journey through Francia with Augustinus, when Tola's safety was in my hands, I saw her grow in self-confidence, marking her out from other women. And with her real desire to help the sick and ailing, I had no doubts that Tola was the one. She has no equal."

"She has a terrible temper sometimes," I cautioned.

"Yes, mostly with fools, Alric," he shot back with a smile.

"I suspected Tola was growing fond of you. She wept when you left for Rome. What I *will* say is that you've both made a great choice!"

We remained silent for a long while, then Cadmon spoke.

"By chance, while I was in Rome, I came across Paulina on my way to the Lateran."

My heart pounded. "She is well?" I asked.

"Yes, she is." Cadmon nodded and pursed his lips, and another silence fell between us. Then he said, "She is married now. One of the workmen—from her parents' old farm."

I nodded. "That's good," I said in a hollow voice.

An even longer silence followed, punctuated only by the sound of the oars dipping in and out of the water.

Almost casually, Cadmon added, "She has a son."

"Oh?" I looked up.

"Yes. A boy. Fifteen months old at the time I saw him."

Then there followed the longest silence of all.

I rowed on steadily, in shock at what I'd heard. I dared not ask and, for a long while, Cadmon said nothing.

"I saw much of you in the child, Alric. And he has your eyes."

*

I returned to Coningsburh and the Abbey in a state of turmoil, burdened by a considerable weight of guilt. I thought of Paulina and the difficulties she must have faced alone, and I shed tears for the child who had my eyes, but whom I would never see. I imagined the life I might have had with Paulina, and my soul was very heavy.

A pile of books and manuscripts filled my desk, selections that Petrus had chosen from the Library at San Andreas, but my pleasure at seeing them remained eclipsed by Cadmon's revelation of my son.

Augustinus entered the Scriptorium, sitting down with a weary sigh.

"These letters," he said, dropping a bundle onto the table. "The first is His Holiness's instructions concerning the financial and organisational matters in the church, on which I wrote to him." He tapped the document with his finger. "Of course, I welcome his wise counsel, as always."

He paused, spreading out two other parchments.

"This one is a copy of a letter that the Pope wrote to the Bishop of Alexandria, singing my praises. He writes that he has received information concerning my ministry here in Cantia, which he describes as being — and I quote — '... *one resplendent with such great miracles that they seem to imitate the very powers of the first apostles in the signs that they display ...*' And a little further on, '*... at the solemnity of the Lord's Nativity in our first year, more than ten thousand Angli were baptised by our brother monk and fellow Bishop, Augustinus.*'"

"Well, that's all encouraging!" I congratulated.

Augustinus shook his head.

"Unfortunately, Alric, it is not. The numbers are heavily exaggerated, as you saw for yourself on the Medd-Wey. I am assuming that Prior Laurentius was responsible for this particular account given to His Holiness."

The Bishop paused, and I sensed he was finally coming to the point.

"However, the last letter to me struck an altogether different tone. The Pope cautions my use of miracles, lest I lose my soul in the doing. But in truth, he seems content with the miracles. I ask you, Alric, what is your opinion? Are you similarly concerned for me? Be honest. Flattery and evasion are of no help to me."

I sat stunned, thinking back to all that had happened from the time of our arrival in Turones, where we had learned of the miracles of San Martinus; and since then, the miracles that had followed at Augustinus's hand in Francia, and now in Cantia also. This was something that neither he nor any of us would have expected. Yet, I had never noted even a hint of arrogance in him.

I measured my words carefully.

"I can truly say, I find you innocent of any charges placed upon you. Without your deeds of power, and without winning the support of Ethelbert, none of what we are doing now would have been remotely possible. No, Bishop, I beg that you rest in peace concerning this matter."

Augustinus sat wrapped in his thoughts, gazing at the letters on the table. "Thank you, Alric, for your candour—and your honesty." Augustinus began to rise.

I sensed it was now or never for me to be fully transparent. And in truth, I was such a bundle of nervous contradictions that I was desperate to share the burden of my heart.

"There is something I must tell you, Bishop," I uttered impulsively.

"What's on your mind, Alric?" Augustinus put the letters into his habit pocket, sat down again and folded his hands, waiting for me to speak.

"When Cadmon returned, he also gave me some personal news from Rome."

"Yes?" he asked encouragingly.

I swallowed hard.

"It transpires ... that I have left behind a son in the Holy City! When we returned from Aquae Sextiae for the letters we needed from Pope Gregorius, Paulina and I met very briefly—and we chanced to meet on the night before we left Rome."

I hung my head in grief and shame, tears finally welling up as I told my tale.

Augustinus asked, "Paulina told this to Cadmon?"

"No. She said nothing of what transpired between us. But Cadmon remarked that the child looked much like me."

There was a long pause, then Augustinus asked, "So where is Paulina now?"

"Still at San Quattro Coronati, Bishop."

"She raises her child alone?"

"No, she married one of the farm workers who fled her father's estate when the Langobards burned everything down. Her husband must know that the child is not his."

"And the child's name?"

"Victorinus."

Augustinus paused in thought, and sighed.

"You are not the first young man to find himself in this position, Alric. But Paulina has married, and they are raising Victorinus together as husband and wife. She has put no obligation upon you?"

I shook my head. "None."

"You are fortunate," he said in a kindly voice. Silence fell between us.

"Do you wish to seek absolution?"

I nodded, wiping my eyes.

"Let us go into the Chapel, and I shall hear your confession there."

We left the chapel a while later to find Queen Bertha's maid waiting patiently for Augustinus. "The Queen urgently wishes to speak with you. Will you come with me, please?"

"We shall go together, Alric," Augustinus said, and we swiftly followed the maid to a reception room within Bertha's quarters. The Queen was deeply troubled.

"I have here a letter from Pope Gregorius that Laurentius brought back from Rome. I find myself confused, surprised, and disappointed by the contents. His Holiness seems to be unaware of how matters have progressed since your arrival last year."

She held the letter out to Augustinus, and he read

some extracts aloud.

'With the goodness of your wisdom, as a true Christian, you should have already inclined the heart of our glorious son your spouse to follow the faith that you cherish for the salvation of his kingdom and his soul. This should have been neither slow nor difficult for you; and since by God's will now is an appropriate time, proceed so that with divine grace cooperating, you can make reparation with an increase for what has been neglected.'

The Queen was indignant.

"But the King made his profession of faith and was baptised more than a year ago! And he has received instruction from you, Bishop, ever since. This is outrageous! Has no one kept His Holiness informed of the progress we've made here? The mission grows apace, a Cathedral is being built, an Abbey is planned, and the poor have good news preached to them. What more does he ask?"

Augustinus was visibly shocked.

"My Lady, I am sure that there must be a mistake in the information that the Pope received. I will make enquiries, but for your part, I advise you to cast this from your mind and think no more of it. Leave it with me. I also think it best that you do not share this with the King. It can only stir up something that is best left buried."

As we walked swiftly through the gates of Coningsburh to our quarters, Augustinus wondered aloud, "Who would have given the Pope this briefing on how matters lie here in Cantia? Who but Laurentius could have described Queen Bertha's Christian influence on her King in such a way that the Pope was compelled to write a rebuke to her?"

The Pope's letter had shown very little grasp of the difficult context and the constraints that the existing pagan beliefs posed. Even the King's baptism had received no mention.

Augustinus met privately with Laurentius soon afterwards. The Scriptorium where I was working shared a wooden partition with Augustinus's study, so that I found myself overhearing their conversation. Laurentius had not seen the letter to the Queen; he had merely delivered it.

However, there was yet another issue that our Bishop needed to challenge.

"Here, Laurentius; read this letter that you brought me from Pope Gregorius. What tale did you offer to Pope Gregorius that provoked a response such as this from His Holiness?"

Laurentius, totally unprepared for such a question, was shocked, attempting to bluster his way out on the back of incoherent excuses.

Augustinus also read aloud from the Pope's letter to Queen Bertha.

"Are you suggesting, Laurentius, that the Pope wrote this letter to the Queen *without* hearing your account of the mission? That I cannot believe! And do you realise the damage you might have caused to our crucial relationship with the King, without whose support we have no Cathedral, monastery or mission? I find myself sadly disappointed in you, as someone for whom we had only the highest expectations."

Laurentius attempted to dismiss the Bishop's allegations, but Augustinus pressed on.

"Did you also ask His Holiness to release you from our mission?"

Laurentius gave no reply.

I knew that Laurentius's appointment some years ago, as the Pope's legate to the Emperor's Court, had been a significant step-up for him, exciting high expectations on the part of his patrician family in Rome. It was not unusual for a Papal Legate to be appointed to high office after his return from abroad, and perhaps to be in line for the Papacy when the Pope had passed away.

I heard Augustinus sigh.

"The days when the Church could arrive supported by legions of soldiers and convert the pagans by force, are long since gone, Laurentius. That is not our way. Christ's authority is rooted in suffering and surrendering power, not wielding the whip or the sword. 'God so loved the world, that he gave his only son…' That is strength, Laurentius, not weakness. That is honour, not cowardice. We come with the gift of love—as servants, not enforcers."

A long silence followed.

I thought they must have left the room.

"Do you wish to remain here with us, Laurentius? Or shall I release you from your obligation so that you may return to Rome?"

Laurentius stirred in his chair, and in a voice I scarcely recognised, he finally spoke.

"Bishop, the truth is, I have nowhere else to go."

XII
THE WEDDING RATTEBURG,

Spring, AD 599

IN OUR SAXON Law, there are many contracts verbally entered into that can be acknowledged purely by witnesses. Marriage is one of them.

Cadmon returned to the Haven a few days after proposing to Tola to talk terms with Galen as the father of the bride. It was a great boon to us that our families were well acquainted with each other.

I also returned to the Haven, now old enough to stand as one of the witnesses. Adelmar, one of Cadmon's cavalrymen at Ratteburg served as the other.

First came the discussion of the Morning Gift, an amount to be paid by Pa to Tola on the morning after the wedding, giving her some measure of independence and security; and also to help raise her children should Cadmon desert her, or die from whatever cause. For Cadmon, as a military man, this was always a real possibility.

There was also a gift from the groom to Galen and Erlina, the *handgeld*, to show that he was able to provide for Tola, but also to recompense our family for the notional loss of Tola's labour at the Haven. If something unforeseen should happen to Cadmon, then Galen and Erlina would give Tola her Bridal Dowry. This sum would be Tola's, for her own use as she wished.

However important all this was, by far the most crucial element was Tola's wedding garment. After a lifetime's worth of discussion amongst the women-folk at the Haven, a message arrived from Queen Bertha. Tola eagerly opened the letter, reading aloud an invitation for Mama and Odelinda to visit Coningsburh and help decide on fabrics for the bridal gown and the usual accompaniments. Everything would be a gift from the Queen.

*

The wedding ceremony took place in Sighart's Mead Hall one fine spring day at the end of April. The entire community at the Haven took to the boats and journeyed to Ratteburg for the occasion. Everyone who had accompanied Tola on our long journey from Rome through Francia came to celebrate the day.

My heart still struggled with many mixed emotions as I thought of Paulina in Rome, and the wedding that we might have had if I had known she was with child; but it was not to be. I rejoiced for my sister and Cadmon, and set aside my sadness and regret.

Coifin would usually have officiated at a Saxon marriage ceremony, but Wodin's High Priest was neither invited nor present. Nor, I noted as I scanned the heavens, were the mythical thread-weavers Frigg and her sisters seated at their loom. Instead, Bishop Augustinus conducted the ceremony.

As part of the ritual, Pa presented Cadmon with a sword that our companion Numerius the Hammer had forged in Coningsburh, as a symbol of protection for their home. Sighart presented another shiny blade to Tola, passed down as an heirloom in their family to hand-on one day to their eldest son and heir.

"But don't hesitate to use it if he gives you trouble!" Sighart said to Tola with a wink, and a meaningful glance at his son.

An exchange of rings followed, and Cadmon handed Tola the keys to their new dwelling in the grounds at Ratteburg, signifying that Tola was the undisputed governess of her household.

Next, Cadmon and Tola shared the Loving Cup, and made their toast to the Almighty. At last the feasting was underway, with merriment and toasting for blessings following the marriage.

Much later into the evening came the bride race between our two families, a sprint across to Cadmon and Tola's new home. The groom opened the door, lifted his bride and carried her across the threshold.

Later the following morning, Pa brought over the promised Wedding Gift for the bride, and with that, all was done. Our two families had become as one, with Tola as the peace-weaver and shield-maiden for our two families. An attack on one member would be construed as an attack on the entire family.

In all of this, Cadmon's brother Derian was nowhere to be seen.

"He is no longer part of my family," Sighart had said, and that was the end of the matter.

*

Once an older daughter was betrothed, the gates were thrown open for younger members of the family to follow. My musings on this matter seemed reinforced by the arrival, in the summer of the year AD 599, of a messenger from the Haven.

"You are wanted at Sandwic," he declared.

"Why? What has happened?"

"I don't know that anything has happened," he said. "But your mother has requested that you come without delay."

"I'll come at once. Do you have a boat available?"

"Yes; it's waiting for us at Fordwic."

I walked swiftly from the mooring at the Haven, through the open gate and into our family compound. Erlina and Galen were there, together with Greta and Godric. Only Tola was absent, attending to her obligations at home in Ratteburg. Our family and friends sat in a circle on felled logs, with a large space for an open fire in the centre. Mama called out a greeting to me, and rose to her feet as I approached.

"Mama! I came as soon as I could!"

Looking around, I noticed there was another person present, a tall young woodsman called Aiken who worked with the oaks and hardwoods of the forest. Aiken was one of many orphans raised in our hamlet over the years, usually after the premature death of a mother when the father eventually drifted away unable to cope, leaving his infant behind.

After hugs and kisses, Pa said, "It is good that you could come, Alric! I know how busy you are at the monastery. But you should hear the news from your own family rather than from strangers."

Mama said, "Alric, Aiken has asked for Greta's hand in marriage! Isn't that wonderful!"

This *was* a surprise. I looked in utter confusion at my darling little sister.

"But she's not old enough, Mama!" I blurted out. "She's still a little girl!"

Erlina was indignant. She rose, drawing herself up to her full height.

"Old enough? She's turned fifteen years of age! Before you get on your high horse, my son, let me tell you they will be married when Greta turns sixteen next year. And in case you have forgotten, I married your father when I was fifteen!"

Godric looked on, baring his teeth in a wolf-like grin at my embarrassment.

Thinking swiftly to rescue the situation, I swooped down and lifted Greta in my arms. She squealed in surprise as I gave her a huge hug and kiss on each cheek.

"Congratulations little sister! You couldn't be marrying a finer man!"

I lowered Greta to the ground and extended my hand to Aiken's firm grip, then hugged him too. Everyone was smiling once again.

Mama asked, "Do you think the Bishop will come?"

"I'm sure of it!" I said, crossing my fingers behind my back.

I stayed most of the day while plans were agreed. Another hovel would need to be built soon, and all the legal hurdles addressed. Except that Aiken was an orphan, and had neither a parent nor another family to act for him.

He was like Pa, I thought, and I looked at him with new eyes. He wasn't the kind of man who would walk away from his child. I thought of my own son in Rome; Aiken was a better man than I.

Then, partly because there was no one else, but mostly because I respected him as honest, strong and hardworking, I rose to my feet and raised my hand.

"*I* will stand on behalf of Aiken's parents!"

*

The following year Tola was safely delivered of a daughter. She named her child Erlina, after our mother, and that seemed to please everyone.

I sat at Tola's bedside as she cuddled little Erlina, and thought of Paulina and our son, who I would have loved to hold in my arms and whisper to him how wonderful he was.

I asked Tola a question that had long been on my mind.

"Tola, when Cadmon came back from Rome and asked for your hand, what were you arguing about? I was certain, from all the noise you two were making, that you'd said no!"

Tola smiled. "It was her," she said, looking down at baby Erlina rocking gently in her arms.

I looked at Tola, puzzled. She said,

"Cadmon had just returned from another adventure, you remember? For months, I didn't know if he was dead or alive, the same as Mama and Papa didn't know what had happened to us in

Rome and Francia. I couldn't go through that again, Alric. I just couldn't. I said to him, 'I'm not having you give me babies and go away on your jaunts, leaving me struggling on my own; and you, never home long enough for your children to know who you are!'"

"That was some risk," I said with a half laugh. "What did he say?"

"He said he would never go away again, at least until we had raised our children, and probably not even then. He was tired of adventure. A family of his own was what he truly wanted. You know him—he would never lie about something as important as this. I do believe he meant it. So I said yes."

Later, I walked away from their dwelling and took a few deep breaths of wind coming off the sea, feeling that gradually the deep wounds of separation during our seven lost years were finally being washed away. In the marrow of my bones also, I felt the old settled order was changing, but I could not tell how.

I took in another deep breath, straightened my back with fresh resolve, and walked swiftly to the boat straining at its moorings, strangely eager for the next challenge.

XIII

NEW FACES FROM ROME

AD 601 - 603

BY EARLY SPRING in 601 Queen Bertha was with child, and given her age, the large gap between her two sons and the new birth was potentially dangerous for her as a mother. In the event, there was nothing to fear, and the Queen was delivered of a healthy babe whose name, Ethelburga, was a combination of 'Ethelbert' and Bertha's mother, 'Ingoburga'; a young sister to the older princes, Eadbald and Ethelwald.

Soon afterwards, a fourteen-year-old girl from a noble family in Francia arrived to support the Queen and her newborn child. Her name was Gisela, the daughter of Count Gundoland, a nobleman from Parisius. Gisela could understand every word we spoke, both in Latin and Saxon. With her quick mind, she soon learned what she did not know.

None of us could foresee the part that Gisela would one day play in the unfolding—and the unravelling—of the Kingdom of Cantia.

*

In the summer of the same year, five new arrivals joined our community, sent from Rome by Pope Gregorius.

Abbot Petrus stood in the doorway of my study.

"Come Alric. They are here!"

We gathered in the Chapel for a prayer of thanksgiving for their safe arrival, and afterwards, Augustinus warmly welcomed the newcomers to our community at the midday meal in our Refectory. Abbot Mellitus, a learned man who had served as Abbot of San Andreas, rose to respond to Augustinus. Once the introductions were completed, Mellitus placed a carefully wrapped gift into Augustinus's hands.

"From His Holiness, for all that you have achieved here in a few short years!"

Augustinus expressed his thanks and carefully opened the slim wooden box, taking out a Y-shaped pallium to be worn beneath his garments when celebrating the Mass. The accompanying letter from the Pope was deeply moving, declaring that Augustinus was now Archbishop within all of Ethelbert's territories.

As we settled down to eat, I observed each of our new arrivals. In time, I would know them in more depth, but for the moment Abbot Mellitus had come as the leader of the party from Rome—not on account of his tall stature and broad girth, nor his permanent half-smile similar to Bishop Augustinus, but on account of his warm and willing demeanour.

Justus looked somewhat like Laurentius in his severe black cassock, but soon turned out to be quite a different character: congenial, welcoming, thoughtful and willing to try new ideas. He had also scoured for books, at San Vincentius Monastery in Massilia, interested to convert pagan animal sacrifices into Christian feasts.

Paulinus, also a priest, was the third member of this group from Rome chosen by Gregorius. Preaching and teaching were still seen as the work of the clergy rather than by the monks. Paulinus was younger than he first appeared, on account of his thick grey hair combed forward in the traditional Roman manner, and of course tonsured, as were all our clergy and monks.

A fourth member, Nathaniel, also from San Andreas Monastery, was a young monk with a quiet manner, and said to be noted for his probity.

Lastly, Brother Honorius from San Andreas completed our group of new companions—youthful, shorter in stature than many, and eager to make his mark.

All of them were clean-shaven, something that bearded Saxons would draw attention to; and all of our welcome new arrivals lacked an understanding of the religion, the culture and the values of our Saxon people.

*

Augustinus called us together in the Chapel after breakfast, and began by asking Mellitus, "You mentioned that the Pope's views on how to evangelise the pagans in Cantia have now changed. How so? This is both unexpected and intriguing."

Mellitus explained, "The Pope's earlier approach to converting people to the Faith was to compel local pagan kings and rulers to adopt the Christian faith; but now the Pope suggests that the conversion of the Saxons be undertaken gradually, by transforming pagan rituals and customs into Christian ones, particularly at major festivals."

Augustinus smiled. "I think the Pope would be relieved to know that, from the outset, this has been the approach we have adopted here in Cantia. It is good that we share a common mind in this matter."

Forceful a character as the King was, even he would not have lasted a week had he ignored the beliefs of his Cantwara people.

Later that morning the King summoned Augustinus and me to his chambers. Augustinus seldom failed to pause and exchange a few words of greeting and encouragement with whoever was on duty. The guards at the gate were well acquainted with us, and we addressed them all by name.

Seated in our customary meeting place, Bertha handed over her young child Ethelburga to her nursemaid. Gisela walked up and down at the rear of the room, slowly rocking the babe as our meeting began.

Ethelbert commanded, "Read the letter from the Pope to us! First, let me hear how it sounds in Latin. Alric, you translate."

Augustinus handed me the letter Mellitus had given him the previous day, and I read out, "*In Domino gloriosissimo, atque præcellentissimo filio Ethelberto regi Anglorum, Gregorius episcopus ...*"

"To the most glorious lord, and his most excellent son, Ethelbert, king of Cantia, from Bishop Gregorius..."

The Pope addressed Ethelbert in the most flattering terms: he was 'his most excellent son', 'my illustrious son', and the Pope's icon for Ethelbert to aim for was no less than the first Christian Emperor, Constantinus Magno.

Beneath all the flattery, it was an excellent epistle.

Then I translated the second letter.

"Augustinus should not destroy the temples of pagan gods, but only the idols within those temples. He should also purify them with holy water, and in these temples place altars and relics of the saints, because, if those temples are well built, they should be converted from the worship of demons to the service of the true God. This would make it easier for pagans to come to these converted churches to worship God."

The Pope's new strategy for mission went even further. Pagans should no longer sacrifice and eat slaughtered animals as an offering to the devil, but to the glory of God.

Pope Gregorius had also reminded Augustinus that, *"it is impossible in a moment to efface everything from their captive minds. When someone attempts to reach the top of a mountain, he must climb by stages and step by step, not by leaps and bounds."*

To his lasting credit, King Ethelbert had known from the outset that this was the appropriate way to proceed. The Pope's letter was a staggering endorsement of the missionary approach Augustinus had chosen since we arrived. Here, at last, was a common rule for a pagan land. Our time here had not been wasted.

The Queen was all smiles, and so were we.

Gisela returned the infant to her mother as we said our farewells, and I noted that this young Frankish girl had followed every word that had been spoken in Latin in which the letter was written; and in our Saxon tongue that, as a Frank, she understood with ease.

*

Twenty months later, in the year AD 603, with most of the building work for the Cathedral completed, the clergy and lay clerks who had come from Turones and Rome processed down the hill from the old Abbey to occupy their new accommodation at the Cathedral. The living quarters were typical Saxon wood and thatch hovels, clustered close by the Cathedral —in itself a stunning sight, visible from everywhere within and beyond the walls of Cantwaraburh.

Building work on the new Abbey could now proceed apace.

With more accommodation freed-up in our former Abbey at San Martinus's Chapel, the numbers of young Saxon boys entering our school increased.

I returned as often as I could to visit my family at the Haven, and Tola at Ratteburg, seldom visiting the one without seeing the other. Tola was happier than I could have imagined, now expecting her second child. Cadmon's Cavalry School drew widespread attention, groups of fifteen at a time spending a few months together at Ratteburg to improve their horsemanship and combat skills. Seven of the Earls of the Realm had sent their young Thanes to Cadmon's Academy. Only the Earl of Rofesburh failed to recognise the value of Cadmon's training. He warned, "We haven't had a war in my lifetime. Our swords and javelins are no more than ornaments."

And yet, I observed, despite continued peace in the Kingdom, both King and Archbishop seemed restless. Eventually Augustinus confided in me. "Ethelbert's ambitions are not confined to the Kingdom of Cantia, Alric, and his reputation amongst many of the Saxon Kingdoms remains widely accepted. What he has done these last few years is not enough for him; we both believe he can achieve more. You remember that in the Pope's letter he recognises the King's important role—both in our mission, but also through his sense of destiny?"

I nodded. "Are you thinking of the Pope's words comparing him to Emperor Constantinus?"

"I am. The Pope stirred his ambitions. The King expects he might yet be overlord over *all* Saxons—including the kingdoms of the north. And he also wants to be free from any suggestion that he is beholden to that yapping pup, King Chlothar of Neustria."

"And as for you, Bishop? What stirs in you?"

After a long pause, Augustinus finally answered.

"Ethelbert's overlordship presently includes the conquered Saxon province of the Hwicce, an area to the far west containing a considerable British remnant, but whose coexistence is unusually friendly. Perhaps through them, a Roman Church with all the authority of the Pope supporting it, could have a strong claim upon the loyalties of the British Church in the lands to the far west? Should we not also draw them into the influence of both Cantia and Rome? Would that be acceptable to them?"

He paused. "The prize would be to bring the British Church into the Catholic Church, as a partner, in leading all the Saxon Kings into the Kingdom of Christ. With Ethelbert's overlordship widely acknowledged, and the Church planted in the Saxon Kingdoms, that is surely a prize worth striving for!"

*

The following day Augustinus called me to his study.

"The King has made up his mind. He wants me to speak with the British Bishops. Come, Alric, there's much to do. We leave in three weeks!"

Before we set out on our journey to the west, Augustinus consecrated Laurentius as a Bishop to ensure succession in the event that he failed to return. Our still-fragile mission in these early years should not falter for want of a Shepherd.

Augustinus handed to Laurentius the Pope's letter concerning how the Church should be ordered. It was up to Laurentius now, as a superb administrator, to handle such matters. Laurentius had shown talent in his time at the Imperial Court in Constantinople, and also as Prior in Gregorius's monastic community at the Lateran.

With the prospect of the King leaving his Kingdom, possibly for several months, every precaution needed to be taken against efforts to seize the Kingdom in Ethelbert's absence. Waeslinga Stract was closed to travellers coming from Wessex, and squadrons of Cadmon's cavalrymen controlled every entry point. All the seaports and river access points were secured, and warriors were posted at strategic places on the coast—as well as around the Wantsum Channel, and the Medd-Way River at Rofesburh.

*

Earl Sighart and Odelinda prepared to move from Ratteburg to Coningsburh and await the King's return. All the Kingdom's Earls were informed that Sighart was given charge of the Kingdom's *fyrd* for the duration of Ethelbert's absence. Queen Bertha remained in Coningsburh with her young daughter Ethelburga, her two sons, and Gisela. Cadmon rowed his heavily pregnant wife and their young daughter Erlina across to the Haven. A squadron of five of Cadmon's horsemen was stationed at our family compound, with the gate to the quay always under guard.

But Tola was annoyed; not least because Cadmon seemed about to break the promise he made her before their marriage.

"Cadmon, why are you bringing me back to the Haven?"

"Because you might not be safe at Ratteburg. My father and mother have moved to Coningsburh until the King returns. Look, you are about to give birth. Better for you and our child to be with our family at a time like this. My cavalrymen will protect you, and everyone else at the Haven, that I promise you."

A signal-pyre was erected on the shingle at the fishing village of Stonar, across the narrow Estuary from the Haven, and made ready to send a warning signal, alerting both Ratteburg and Raculf, should warships suddenly appear from the sea. The port of Dubris was similarly guarded. In short, we displayed the same feverish intensity of any Kingdom preparing for war.

In the event, there would be a war, certainly; but not the conflict we had expected.

XIV
TURN OF THE TIDE
THE BRITISH CHURCH
Late 603 AD

WITH ITS MAINSAIL unfurling, the King's warship at Fordwic drifted into the middle of the river. Standing in the prow with our King and Archbishop I glanced at Mellitus, Justus and Paulinus, wondering how they would fare on this expedition. Laurentius, newly consecrated as Bishop, remained behind at Cantwaraburh to oversee the Cathedral. Cadmon and four cavalrymen travelled with us to protect our overland journey from Lundenwic to the Kingdom of the Hwicce.

Tola was not well pleased, but the Kingdoms on our route were not said to be hostile, and there was little likelihood of conflict on the journey. I had expected that Prince Eadbald, as next in line to the throne, might have joined us to widen his knowledge of the Saxon kingdoms, but he was not on board ship. Although he regularly attended the Mass along with his parents and younger brother, Eadbald's interests lay elsewhere.

*

Our route took us past the fort of Raculf, where Ethelbert as Prince had fought for his life and his crown against Hrothgar on the day after King Eormenric's burial. Vivid memories of those few days came flooding back as we anchored at Raculf to pass the night in a ghostly, empty Royal Hall.

Here, Felix had received payment from Darien to seize Cadmon, sparking a series of events that led to the three of us being snatched away from the Haven, for seven long years. Earl Sighart was still unaware of this transaction, but it had cost Cadmon, Tola and me very dearly. I shuddered as though an icy finger had drawn down my spine, and I caught Cadmon's eye as our warship came near to the landing-place.

Before gathering in the lonely Hall, we walked down to the shore and stood in silence at the burial site that once contained King Eormenric's body. Here the restless sea had reclaimed him as it's own. Nothing remained of our departed King's ship; the tide had broken into the stone-and-earth burial mound, pounding the mast and planking to splinters, dragging out the King's weapons, shield, gold rings—and the bones of Eormenric himself.

Ethelbert knelt on the shore at King Eormenric's last resting-place, and signalled for Augustinus to join him.

"The King's body is long since gone, washed out on the tide; but could you pray for him? I can still sense here his unquiet soul."

Come the morning we sailed westward, keeping land in sight until we reached the mouth of the broad Medd-Way Estuary. We anchored close by the bridge that carried Waeslinga Straet over to the western bank where the ancient cobbled road continued towards Lundenwic, some thirty miles further west. The Earl of Rofesburh's Mead Hall stood just outside the walls of the old Roman castrum. The Earl welcomed us dutifully but did not hide his scepticism of our mission.

Later, during the evening meal, the Earl turned to me and said, "What about you, Alric? What's your speciality?"

"My Lord, I teach young lads to read and write; a great boon for good management of the estates."

The Earl scoffed, neither impressed nor interested.

"You do realise, Alric, there is great danger in allowing young men to think they know more than their superiors!"

I smiled politely and shrugged, thinking, can it be that this old fool is all that stands between the warriors of the West Saxons and us in Cantwaraburh? He refuses to train his cavalry, and he cannot read the runes, even if someone scribbled them on his wall!

In the morning Ethelbert declared to his startled Earl, "We shall soon need a church here for Bishop Justus, set close by this road so that worshippers have both easy access to it, and also for the protection of Rofesburh. We'll begin the building work after I return. In the meantime, we give you our thanks for your generous hospitality!"

*

We set sail for Lundenwic in the far west corner of the Kingdom of the East Saxons, a place that I had never travelled to before. Excitement ran through me as the ancient walled Roman town of Londinium came into view.

"Londinium," Ethelbert announced, "is a ruin now, like Cantwaraburh. You will have your work cut out to restore that old Cathedral, Mellitus! And a little further on, do you see—on the north bank?" Ethelbert pointed to the old Roman town. "That's Lundenwic."

As we landed a mile or so further on, King Siebert of Essex, Ethelbert's nephew, hurried down to the quay to greet us. Siebert had not yet made a Christian confession, but the bond of affection between uncle and nephew was nevertheless strong, particularly as Ethelbert was Siebert's Overlord.

The marketplace proved to be typical of other Saxon hamlets on the river—a jetty or two attached to a quay, wood and thatch warehouses close by the water, fishing nets hanging out to dry, hovels scattered about haphazardly, and a large Mead Hall within a fenced compound, marking the residence of the King.

In Siebert's Royal Hall that night I became aware that Siebert's sons, like Ethelbert's, had no interest in the new religion, and preferred pagan ways. But Siebert had other worries.

"King Penda of Mercia makes for an uncomfortable neighbour," he said. "Penda is an ambitious man, a restless warrior who wants to dominate *all* the Saxon kingdoms, from Cantia to Hadrian's Wall!"

Ethelbert put a hand on Siebert's shoulder.

"Keep your sword sharp, Siebert. Send out scouts to patrol your borders. Take no chances, and prepare your warriors well. I also sense that times are changing."

*

In the morning, leaving our ship and crew moored at Lundenwic, we made preparations to depart for Corinium. Siebert gave us directions and a guide to the former Roman town, now the chief city of the Hwicce, some sixty miles journey ahead.

"Your best course is to take the road north, then west. Follow the old road known as Akeman Street."

With Cadmon's cavalry, and our guide for protection, we set off following the road Siebert had indicated on a journey that would take several days.

Ethelbert mused aloud, "What are Mercia's intentions concerning this disputed territory? We may have to contend with Penda ourselves, if matters worsen."

The tribal Kingdom of the Hwicce, bounded by the Kingdom of the West Saxons to the south and Mercia to the north, had been established a quarter of a century earlier, after the Battle of Deorham. Ethelbert reminisced, "I fought there for the Hwicce's independence from the West Saxons. This was where Hrothgar's brother fell in battle, slain by an arrow between his shoulders. Now two brothers, Eanhere and Eanfrith, rule this Kingdom. Both are Christians, converted from paganism by Irish monks."

"Well, you might have saved us our long journey from Rome if these Irish monks had travelled east to reach Cantia!" Augustinus teased.

"Yes, but then I would never have had the pleasure of meeting you!" Ethelbert grinned, and I could see their mutual regard was genuine.

"Besides, having the Irish monks come to us in Cantia would not have been acceptable. My Queen is a Catholic; she looks to Francia for her family, her culture and her religion. So, Archbishop, it might have been possible to convert our Saxon people—if my Queen had been Irish, or even British; but not as a Merovingian Frank. That's why we made our request to Francia and Rome for a mission."

"Yes, we came in response to your call from Cantia. But now, O King, I can see that what we have come to these Isles for is much, much greater. We have come in search of *all* the kingdoms!"

*

At the former Roman town of Corinium, we were greeted warmly in the Royal Hall. King Eanhere and his brother, King Eanfrith, had both fought alongside Ethelbert for the freedom of this small Kingdom. As the mead of friendship flowed, Eanhere explained how matters had developed since their last battle against the Saxons of Wessex.

"The Hwicce people, as you know, King Ethelbert, were already converted to faith in Christ by Irish monks when we Saxon pagans first arrived here. Later, we were absorbed into the Irish-British Church, and now we live together in peace. Almost everyone in our kingdom, Saxon and British, confesses Christ here."

Augustinus narrowed his eyes attempting to visualize this—a Church comprising both Saxon and British Christians living in peace, and tolerant of pagan religions.

"This may be the finest example of Christians living in harmony together that I am ever likely to see," he said.

I noticed, above the heads of the two Kings, a pair of shields hanging on the wall. One was a painted emblem of a dragon, the other a painted lion, two mortal enemies that now lived in harmony. I wondered how the Roman Church might achieve this balance, and whether Papal pressures and expectations would hinder the prospects of a united Church, embracing both Catholic and British Churches.

Ethelbert raised some of his own concerns, bringing my own thoughts back to the present. He said to our hosts, the two Kings, "We have passed through three Kingdoms on our journey here. As overlord, I have listened to the same story over and over again, that the West Saxons are attempting to extend dominance over this and other kingdoms that seem vulnerable. The Mercians are restless for war, of this we can be sure, and that will not be to the advantage of either pagan or Christian. For the sake of peace, we ask you to arrange a meeting between us and the British Bishops to discuss these matters together, in the hope that we can find common cause and united action."

On Eanfrith's advice, we agreed that the fishing hamlet of Aust would be a convenient location for the British Bishops to travel to from their respective monasteries. With arrangements finally made to meet the British Bishops, we rode west and installed ourselves in modest accommodation, close by the tidal waters at Aust. A wooden jetty extended into the water where a ferry carried travellers to the opposite bank of the river, some two miles distant. Between high and low tides, the river rose and fell more than forty feet.

The meeting was set to take place on the clifftop, beneath an ancient oak tree.

*

On the day of the gathering we waited on the cliff top, keeping watch for the boat that would ferry the British Bishops to us. Cadmon was the first to see the vessel leave the far shore. As the boat drew nearer, I could see the Bishops tightly cloaked against a cold wind. Augustinus walked down to greet them, exchanging a kiss of peace, and hearing their Roman-British names for the first time. King Ethelbert stepped forward, greeting each one in turn. It seemed a good and amicable beginning as everyone walked up the steep slope to the clifftop.

Speaking in the Latin tongue, Augustinus welcomed the Bishops and explained, "We are most grateful, responding as you have done to our letter my brothers, respectfully requesting a meeting with you for the sake of the Kingdom of God. We have a dual purpose in requesting this meeting with you today. I believe we have a common cause in our calling to extend the faith of Christ throughout this whole land. For this reason, I urge you, with all brotherly affection, that together we can seek and preserve the universal peace of Christ, and undertake our joint task of evangelising the heathen.

"But also, as you know, most of the land in these Isles is under the heel of pagan princes. King Ethelbert, a Christian by conversion six years ago, is the Overlord of territories from the Kingdom of Cantia to the River Humbre. Some of you will know that he fought twice for the freedom of the Hwicce, even when he was not a follower of Christ. We have learned on our journey to you that there is unrest between the Saxon kingdoms, and a fear of war that may even reach yours. That course can be changed with your support in converting the Saxon people to become citizens of a heavenly, peaceable Kingdom. Now, my brothers, what say you?"

After a short silence, several conversations began amongst the British contingent. One of the Bishops raised a question concerning a long-standing difference between the Universal and the British Church.

"How can we respectfully engage together in search of an adequate understanding of God's purposes when there are so many points of difference between us?"

A lengthy dispute followed, but despite the prayers, exhortations and chidings on the part of Augustinus and our companions, the Bishops were unwilling to give their assent. In short, they preferred to keep to their own traditions.

Late in the afternoon Augustinus said, "Let us pray that God, who makes us be of a common mind in his kingdom, will show us a heavenly sign by which we shall know which tradition is to be followed, and by what pathways. So, let a sick man be brought before us. Let the faith and practice of the person who heals him by his prayers be accepted to be in accord with God's will, and let it be right that we should follow!"

The British Bishops readily agreed, and a blind man of the Saxons who lived nearby was led by the hand and brought to the British bishops. Pray as they might, the blind man was not healed, nor did he seem improved in any way. Augustinus came forward to this confused and blind man, and knelt before him, praying fervently that our Lord Christ would restore the man's lost sight so that through the opening of one man's eyes, he might bring the grace of spiritual light into the hearts of many.

Augustinus placed his hands over the fellow's eyes, and his sight was restored at once. All the British Bishops acknowledged that Augustinus was a true herald of the Lord of Light, although some believed it was merely a trick for Augustinus to have his way. However, the British Bishops requested a second conference, when more of their number could attend.

As their boat drew away from the land, Ethelbert astutely remarked, "They are playing for time. They have no serious intention of working together with us to preach to the Saxon kingdoms. The British Bishops are too content, tucked away in their mountain Kingdoms, and do not realise the danger they are placing themselves in!"

Augustinus was exhausted. The long journey and a testing meeting had taken its toll, and his disappointment and failure began to sap his strength. He turned away, with a single cough. From that moment, his strength began to deteriorate.

*

We remained at Aust awaiting the British Bishops' return. All the while Augustinus's condition worsened. With his persistent cough, he rested often to recoup his strength.

While we waited, a messenger arrived, bringing bad news

from King Eanfrith. The messenger said, "A short while ago, at a place called the Stone of Degsa, Aidan, who was inaugurated as King by Columba of Iona, and with an immensely strong army including the Scots of Dal Riata, engaged in battle with the pagan King Ethelfrith of Bernicia. Despite King Aidan's advantage in numbers, King Ethelfrith ravaged the Britons with great savagery. King Aidan has been defeated—he managed to flee with only a handful of survivors."

A shiver ran through me; our time here wasn't going at all well. Cadmon and I exchanged glances.

"And so the story unfolds," Ethelbert murmured.

After much discussion, we decided to request that King Eanfrith and Colum, the Irish monk who had arranged our meeting with the British Bishops, join us for our second meeting at Aust. Augustinus dictated a letter to put before the two kings in Corinium concerning the substance of our meeting with the British Bishops.

"King Ethelbert and Archbishop Augustinus request your presence at our second meeting if that is at all possible. It seems that the British Bishops have a great fear—and an even greater hatred—for the Saxon heathen, constraining them from uniting with us to preach to the Saxons. However, here in your Kingdom, there is ample evidence that this goal is achievable."

The messenger placed the letter in his pouch and galloped back to Corinium.

As we returned to our room, Cadmon and I shared our thoughts concerning how this expedition was faring.

"Between you and me, Alric, I think our next meeting is redundant. It would be better if we took Bishop Augustinus back home at once; but it's not my decision."

"Perhaps there is still time," I said; but I could not even convince myself.

*

Weeks passed before word came that the British Bishops were ready to meet again. King Eanfrith, his Irish priest Colum and his monks came to join us, as they had promised. Augustinus, increasingly ill and frail, took his seat under the oak tree.

This time a much larger contingent of the British arrived, chiefly from their famous Bancornaburg monastery. Aaron, a member of the British aristocracy and leader among the British Bishops, opened proceedings, addressing Augustinus.

"As we set out for this meeting-place here under the oak, we met first with a certain hermit whom we hold in high esteem, to consult with him whether we ought to forsake our traditions as Bishop Augustinus seems to suggest. His answer was, 'If he is a man of God, follow him. If he is harsh and proud, it follows that he is not from God and we have no need to regard his words because he is manifestly not meek and lowly of heart.'"

He paused, and silence fell over the assembled gathering.

"If you were to fail to rise to greet us, Archbishop Augustinus, this would be a sign that you could not be trusted. And so it has proved to be!"

A roar of agreement rose for the words of their Bishop, mixed with outrage so that nothing intelligible could be discerned for several minutes.

Augustinus had remained seated, not to claim superiority but for one significant reason, his increasing infirmity. He shook his head but made no defence. If the British contingent could not see his poor state of health with their own eyes, the words of his mouth would only seem a hasty and spurious defence. Cadmon was right; the British had come to the meeting with no intention of uniting with us.

After several attempts to receive a hearing, Augustinus finally managed a few words.

"What His Holiness Pope Gregory seeks above all things is not dominance, nor your territories, but your commitment—so that in these Last Days the whole Church in these Isles may live peaceably in Christian fraternity. My brothers, spiritual elitism—whether practised in a cave or a monastery, is not 'sharing the Gospel'. I give you the example of Abbot Columbanus, whom we met on our journey from Rome to Cantia."

The mention of Columbanus took the British Bishops completely by surprise. Columbanus, the Irish monk we had met briefly in Francia, was well versed in the Scriptures and reputedly a miracle-worker.

"The ascetic life of the monastery must make way for preaching the scriptures for the salvation of the pagan, who knows no way to make peace except the peace of death by bloodshed. Do we not all believe that there is power in the Word of God? What we need most are preachers and teachers. Look! Here beside me sit two Saxon kings, both Christians, living in peace with their neighbours, worshipping the one God, as I know you do. This itself is a miracle of the Spirit! And alongside the Saxons of the Hwicce live Irish monks who brought to them the Christian message of our sovereign God. Let us be bold, and work together to reach the hearts of the heathen and bring them closer to the throne of heaven."

*

Without a doubt, we witnessed something disturbing and strange that day. These Bishops and scholars employed all their intellectual arguments to avoid working together with us, rather than finding a way of preaching to the Saxons. The bitter enmity that existed between Saxon and Briton had already endured well over a hundred years. They had passed their judgment on the sins of the Saxons, and this side of Hades, as they believed, there was no forgiveness. Despite our Lord's command to go forth and baptise the whole world, the British contingent adamantly refused to preach the Word. Nothing more could be achieved.

With Cadmon supporting Augustinus's one arm and me the other, our Archbishop staggered to his feet. Now it became plain for all to see why he had not arisen when the British Bishops and Scholars arrived, but by now it made no difference.

In a much-weakened voice, Augustinus said, "I know it is said that you do many things contrary to the customs of the universal Church. Nevertheless, if you are willing to accept these three points, we will gladly take no issue with your practices. These three points are clear: to keep Easter at the time that is recognised in the wider Church; to perform the sacrament of baptism for salvation, according to the rites of the universal Church; and in fellowship with us, preach the Word of the Lord to the Saxon people."

A cry came from the British, "We will accept none of your three conditions! Nor will we accept you as our Archbishop! As you were unwilling to arise when we came, how much more will you despise us later if we agree to your terms?"

Augustinus, scarcely audible against the noise and shouting, begged for silence one last time.

"We have, only recently, received news that the Irish King Aidan of Iona has, a short while ago, engaged in battle with the forces of the Saxon King Ethelfrith. I am told that only a handful of Aidan's men have escaped alive."

A hush fell upon the Bishops and theologians, standing ready to depart.

"Be aware, my brothers, that if together we do *not* preach the Way of Life to these pagan Saxons, we risk instead suffering the way of death at their hands."

XV

THE PASSING

603-608 *AD*

AFTER OUR FAILURE to agree with the British Bishops at the end of the year, we returned downhearted to the Cathedral at Cantwaraburh. Augustinus, now frail and sick, called for Bishop Laurentius and without delay consecrated Mellitus as Bishop of Lundenwic in the province of the East Saxons, and Justus as Bishop of Rofesburh. After these two episcopal consecrations, Augustinus had no strength left to celebrate the Nativity. He remained confined to his quarters, where I visited him almost daily.

At Bertha's request, Tola and her children took up temporary residence in the Queen's apartments. Tola attended daily at Augustinus's bedside to alleviate his suffering. Bertha's nursemaid Gisela took charge of Tola's children, in addition to Bertha's daughter Ethelburga, and Tola's friendship with Gisela blossomed.

"She is such a lovely person, Alric," Tola confided. "I hope she finds the right person for her in our Kingdom. It would be a loss if she didn't."

From Coningsburh on the hill to the Cathedral within the walls of Cantwaraburh, a solemn mood descended on us all. Whenever possible, Ethelbert sat with Augustinus, sometimes reminiscing together, but mostly Augustinus coughed with little slumber.

*

In May of 604 Augustinus passed into the next life, and like many, I found myself bereft. He had been a father-figure to me. I remembered the fateful day in Rome when he rescued Cadmon and me from the slave market, and opened a new world of possibilities for us.

After our Archbishop's funeral I was adrift, finding it difficult to concentrate on my teaching and scribing. Tola and the children prepared to return to Ratteburg. "Come back with us, Alric. You need a rest." With a little persuasion, I accompanied her to stay for a few days respite.

Cadmon felt the loss of Augustinus equally keenly, and we walked and talked our way around the Ratteburg estate, remembering how we first met Augustinus.

"I liked him right straight away," I said. "There was nothing artificial about him. Despite our difference in age and status, he never put me down, never ridiculed. He always listened and had a wise answer. But who can we look to now?"

"Unfortunately, I see none of Augustinus's qualities in Laurentius," Cadmon said, shaking his head. "I cannot fathom why the Pope chose him for the mission—arrogant, harsh and self-seeking, always opposing Augustinus. You have a nightmare on your hands now, Alric!"

Tola chastised me after I returned from our walk.

"You can't remain like this forever Alric," she pointed out. "The story's not over yet, hold on to that thought."

A message from the Queen awaited me on my return to our Abbey of San Martinus, and I made my way through the gate to her apartments. I sat down, and Bertha patted my hand reassuringly.

"I wanted to speak with you privately, Alric. I know how hard this time has been for you. I am truly sorry, but you did all that you could. No one could have saved Augustinus from the fate that awaited him. His time had come; now others—including you—

must carry his vision forward. Augustinus had enormous regard for you, not only as a scribe but because you were attentive and supportive, a true friend. His task is done, but yours is not. Take heart, dear Alric, take heart!"

I returned to the Abbey that afternoon to continue my teaching. One of the three boys in the final year adopted a well-known stalling tactic, one that Cadmon and I had used a few times with Abbot Petrus in Rome.

"Grammaticus, you must have known Archbishop Augustinus well, after so many years! How did you meet him? What was he like?"

His question took me off-guard, my feelings still raw. I managed to hold back tears and sat down at the table together with my students. I shared with them the whole story that took Cadmon and me from the Haven to Rome and our return through Francia to Cantia. There was not a dry eye when I had finished, least of all mine, and I became aware how much these boys had grown in learning and understanding these last three years.

"This isn't just a story, it's a legend," the oldest of the three said; and I realised that every word I had spoken to them, and every word I heard from them was in Latin.

Shortly after my session with our students, King Ethelbert called a meeting with his three bishops—Laurentius, Mellitus and Justus. Laurentius had scarcely made any progress in his grasp of Saxon, and our missionaries from Rome had not received sufficient exposure to the language to hold a conversation; so once again I was present as an interpreter.

I sensed that Laurentius would have preferred a private meeting with Ethelbert, but he had not accompanied us to the Kingdom of the Hwicce and had no personal insights into how matters had turned out.

The King began, "I deeply mourn our Archbishop's passing. I want to assure you that he did everything he possibly could in our two meetings at Aust, but the British Bishops and their Abbots, their hermits and scholars, were in no mood to join us for the prize of a united Church—or a unified Kingdom."

The prize of Ethelbert's dynasty, extending his influence as Overlord far wider than military campaigns, had now slipped through his hands. Ethelbert added, "Other kingdoms will have watched and assessed the outcome of our meetings for themselves. I will do what I can while I still have influence, but—for the moment—our grand, visionary scheme is regrettably over."

*

In September we received news of yet another great sadness. Our beloved Pope Gregorius, the architect of our mission, had passed away on March 12th, two months before Augustinus. However, communication with Rome was never easy, and at Cantwaraburh the news of his passing did not reach us until autumn. The Pope's passing was a great blow to us, but that was by no means the end of bad news from Rome.

By mid-September, we also learned that Sabinianus had succeeded Gregorius to the Throne of San Petro the Apostle. Even though Sabinianus had been notably unsuccessful as Envoy to Constantinople, he was nevertheless elected Pope as Gregorius's successor. It was said he had actively supported the anti-monastic faction that had plagued Gregorius after his election as Bishop of Rome. The mood in the Holy City turned against monks holding key positions in the Lateran Palace. Sabinianus also withheld the pallium from Laurentius, who had served Gregorius as his Prior in the Lateran Palace.

Where, we wondered, would that leave us in this still very delicate stage of our mission in the Kingdom of Cantia?

Bishop Laurentius was highly effective as a Cathedral administrator and liturgist, but he had neither the skills nor the interest to extend the mission beyond Cantwaraburh. Mission now fell to his priests who had come from Turones, and Wulfrun their leader was both skilled and eager to continue Augustinus's work. However, both age and health had begun to take its toll.

For my part, I kept my head down, translated for the King when he needed me, concentrated on teaching my students, and let time pass by.

*

Nearly three years had passed when one day, towards the end of June in the year 607, Abbot Petrus came to see me.

"I shall be away for a little while Alric," he informed me. "Our King has commissioned Bishop Justus and me to attend King Chlothar's Council in Parisius next month. I would prefer to let this pass without my participation, but as it may concern a shift in Frankish policy towards the Kingdom of Cantia, it seems wisest to accept."

"Oh? What's that scoundrel up to now?" I asked.

Petrus sat down to explain what he saw unfolding.

"The Franks' Royal Commission could lose us our much-treasured independence. You know how keen they are to keep Cantia as their vassal state. It may be mere speculation, but King Ethelbert sees this Council as an attempt to formally accept Chlothar's overlordship of the Kingdom of Cantia."

I sighed. "Other than refusing to accept Chlothar's overlordship, what other reason would there be for you going?" I pressed.

"Well, first, if we are threatened by war, the Franks would come to our aid."

I laughed out loud. "Come now, Abbot, we journeyed through Francia together! We sampled the so-called 'assistance' offered by their King, forcing Cadmon to join in his war against the Austrasians! With all the military training Cadmon has put into our warriors these last seven years, Cantia is in a stronger military position than anywhere north of Parisius! We don't need Frankish boots on our soil!"

Petrus conceded, "Well, no doubt the main beneficiaries will, as usual, be Count Warnachar and other Mayors of their Palaces."

"And secondly?"

"The other has to do with the Law. Specifically, Ethelbert's Law Code, the *Textus Roffensis* that you wrote down in the Saxon tongue. Still a masterpiece, I may add."

I bowed my head just a little in recognition of his kind words.

Petrus continued, "This will strengthen us in shaping King Chlothar's thinking in his Council. As we have a written document, we have more clout than reciting from my unreliable memory. At the least, we will be able to reject those aspects of Frankish Law that are not to our own Kingdom's advantage."

I nodded. "Good! I'll give you a copy to take with you."

"No need, Alric," Petrus smiled. "I already have one!"

*

Months passed without a word from Abbot Petrus, or Bishop Justus; then one morning in October a messenger from Fordwic arrived in a state of great agitation. He said, "I bring news that your Abbot took a ship from Quentovicus to Fordwic, perhaps a month ago. When the ship did not arrive at the next port of call as expected, one of the Market Master's officials was dispatched to investigate. A ship had run aground in a heavy storm, near Ambleat, further up the coast from Quentovicus and Benonia. Everyone drowned, but one body was washed ashore. As he wore a monk's habit and had a wooden cross around his neck, the local priest buried him in the churchyard. Every night afterwards, the local people said that a light shone on the grave, and that the body must be that of a saint."

I felt my eyes stinging, tears welled up, and I swallowed the lump rising in my throat. I managed to ask, "And Bishop Justus?"

"No sign of him. Perhaps he stayed on in Parisius."

I sat back, staring up at the rafters, shaking my head.

"And the crew?"

"No sign of them either. Drowned at sea. The wreckage washed up near the Estuary, and that was all he could say. None survived, that the priest could tell. But the Quentovicus Market Master *was* acquainted with the skipper and his crew. They ran a warehouse on the river. As you have passed through the market a couple of times, you may have come across them? The skipper's name was Felix."

I sat up in shock. Images of Felix from decades ago flashed before my eyes. I brooded on the invisible scar that he had left on Cadmon, Tola and me. The crew's death by drowning seemed to me to be neither an accident nor coincidence, merely justice. But I thought also of the slaves, manacled to their benches, as Cadmon and I had been, unable to escape as torrents of seawater poured into their drowning vessel. Once we too had come close to death in those raging waters off the coast of Francia.

I arose, taking my tears with me, and entered the Chapel of San Martinus to pray.

*

We deeply mourned the death of Petrus, our first Abbot. For the time being, he was interred in the graveyard of the new Abbey until the Chapel was completed.

Before the end of the year Brother John, a Benedictine monk from the Lateran Palace in Rome, and one of the original companions to come to Cantia, followed after Petrus as our Abbot.

One of John's first tasks as Abbot was to take me aside.

"Alric, you haven't made your profession yet, have you?"

I was taken by surprise at the suddenness of his question, and shook my head.

"Don't you think it's about time you did?"

In the brief pause that followed, a great deal of thinking raced through my head. Why had I not raised this with our now-departed Abbot Petrus? There had been plenty of opportunity over recent years, certainly. Was I still unsure of my motives, my needs, or myself? Balancing between two stools, uncomfortable as it was, had always seemed preferable to actually making a commitment—but why?

As always, the question and the answer came back to Paulina. Not committing to taking my vows meant that the door remained open—however narrow the crack—that one-day, some day, somehow, it might still be possible for me to return to Rome, find Paulina and marry her, the two of us living blissfully happy ever after.

I also knew this wasn't realistic. I was deeply committed to the people here, and at the Haven and Ratteburg, and the thought of returning to Rome was emotionally and practically very, very slim.

This time, my head won over my heart. Abbot John was right; my probation period had ended years ago. The time had come for me to take my final vows, and commit myself to Christ and the Church, once and for all.

I looked up, and nodded.

"Good! I'll speak to the Archbishop, and we'll set a date, shall we?"

*

As the Abbey Chapel was still under construction, the ceremony was held in the Cathedral. I was astonished at how many people came—not the handful of supporters and my family I'd expected, but everyone who had arrived with the mission from Rome, and those who came afterwards, the King and his entire household, all our priests, our laymen, Earl Sighart and Odelinda.

Candles blazed and clouds of incense filled the chancel as I was led by the Abbot's hand, following behind the choir with Archbishop Laurentius bringing up the rear. Our monks led the procession, and afterwards sat closely packed on either side of the chancel.

The focus of the ceremony was the Nicene Creed, "I believe in One God …" followed by three solemn vows of religious profession that constituted the climax—to follow Jesus Christ in poverty, chastity and obedience within this community. From that moment, marriage with Paulina was no longer possible. Something welled-up inside me, powerful, emotional, joyous—like the day that Augustinus had laughed and laughed in the Mead Hall at Eastringe. Peace settled on me, and also a sublime experience of love and gratitude that I had never experienced in this way before.

The Bishop preached on the holy life and prayed, concluding the ceremony with a slim god ring and a blessing; and the deed was done.

Brother Martinus, one of my companions from San Andreas in Rome, had taken his vows before we left Rome. We shared our experiences and the strong difference the prayers and vows had made to me in this experience of sublime Grace.

"It felt intoxicating," Martinus said. "And the radiant change it has made in you is remarkable!"

Afterwards, in the throng outside, I hugged Mama and embraced Pa, my siblings Tola, Godric and Greta—and Cadmon, who whispered in my ear, "I always knew you would come through in the end, brother; well done!"

XVI

VICTORINUS

Summer, 610 AD

I BLEW SOFTLY, watching the ink absorb neatly into a sheet of parchment, and glanced up as our Abbey Gatekeeper poked his head around the door of my study.

"Bishop Mellitus has arrived back from Rome!"

During the pontificate of Pope Gregorius, Bonifacius had been a deacon and a valuable member of the Pope's inner cabinet, holding a key position as the Administrator of Papal Patrimonies. After the death of Gregorius, Sabinianus had briefly held the office Pope until Bonifacius IV succeeded him in 608.

The Pope continued to nurture a close connection with our Roman mission in Cantia, and like Pope Gregorius before him, had encouraged monasticism and also ran the Lateran Palace as a monastery.

Mellitus briefly returned to Rome to consult with the Pope on matters affecting the Church in Cantia.

The Gatekeeper was eager to tell me, "The Bishop has brought a group of clergy and monks back with him. And there's also a young lad with them. He's asking to see you."

"Show him in!" I said cheerfully, rising from my chair.

The youngster entered the room. I noticed that he wore a brown habit, and a much-travelled cloak clasped around his shoulders. He smiled, his blue eyes bright and inquiring. I reckoned he was about twelve or thirteen years of age.

"And who might you be, young man?" I inquired in a friendly tone, noticing that in one hand he carried a package, in the other a bundle of clothes, and when he spoke he addressed me in Latin.

"My name is Victorinus," he said.

Victorinus was a common enough name for this to be coincidental, and I brushed it aside.

"And what brings Victorinus to us today?" I enquired.

"My mother asked me to bring this to you," he said, extending his hand to me.

I took the package, glancing at the youngster.

"And who is your mother, Victorinus?"

"My mother's name is Paulina; from the monastery of San Quattro Coronati, in Rome."

I nearly fainted. My heart raced furiously as I steadied myself with one hand on the desk behind me, braced with the knowledge that a year earlier I had taken life vows in our cathedral.

"Please, sit." I motioned him to one of the chairs in front of the desk, and slowly unwrapped the package, tightly packed and tied with several yards of twine. I carefully removed the contents, revealing an old, familiar cloak.

"My mother says that you forgot to take it when you left Rome; you would miss it on cold winter nights."

My mind was racing.

"It will certainly keep me warm!" I managed to say with a forced laugh. "Please, thank your mother for my cloak when you return."

Downcast, Victorinus shook his head. "I have come as a postulant from San Andreas Monastery in Rome, and I'm part of the Pope's mission that arrived today. I'm not expecting to return; I've come to join your Abbey."

My hand was shaking as I poured out two tumblers of water,

handing one to Victorinus. He certainly looked much like his mother as I remembered her, but I wasn't sure what it was about him that looked like me—although Cadmon had once suggested as much, but that was more than a decade ago.

"You have come to join the Abbey," I repeated slowly, like someone talking in his sleep. "Well then, Victorinus, I must take you to meet our Abbot! But first, tell me a little about yourself. Did you choose to come here? Tell me your story."

Later, when he had finished his tale, I said, "Victorinus, you must send a message to your mother at once, letting her know that you have arrived safely. Here, use my desk. There's some parchment, a quill and ink. You should write it straight away, and I'll have it dispatched on the ship that brought you here."

Victorinus wrote carefully in a firm hand. I folded the letter and sealed it with wax. "Come, we'll take this to the Gatekeeper. I'm sure your mother will be relieved that you've arrived safely!"

Later, alone in my study, I reflected on all that Victorinus had said. Paulina did not want her son to be a farmer like all her family before her, as far back as anyone could remember. Coming to Cantia was Victorinus's chance for a new start—as Rome had been for me. Victorinus had said he was about ten years old when Paulina took him to our monastery of San Andreas, less than fifteen minutes' walk from their home, on the San Quattro Coronati estate. Victorinus was accepted as a postulant, and his life followed much the same pattern as mine. And of course, he also learned to read and write in Latin.

Paulina, Victorinus said, had also set her mind to learn to read and write, with the help of a kindly nun at San Quattro. There was also a vital piece of news that Victorinus had mentioned. Paulina was married to Septimus, the chief gardener for their San Quattro Coronati estate, and they had three children. She was married with other children in their family, while I had taken my final vows of celibacy as a monk.

I sighed. All was well.

I carefully unwrapped the package again and pressed the cloak to my face. Paulina had thoroughly cleaned and pressed the garment until it looked almost new. All the same, my thoughts and feelings of that last night in Rome came flooding back, unlocking memories of an orchard in a Roman nunnery on a warm August night, with apples ready for harvest and soft grass beneath the boughs of a tree. Taking one last deep breath, I reluctantly returned the cloak to its wrapping. I had lost Paulina forever, but her son—our son, although he seemed unaware of it—was here with me. I found myself in a dilemma; does Victorinus know? Should I tell him? Or wait and see what happens?

A reply from Paulina arrived a little more than seven months after Victorinus joined our Abbey. He did not show me the letter, but I learned from him that his mother and the family were well. Rome, she wrote, was still a city surrounded by enemies, yet somehow life went on, and she was glad my cloak had been returned; and that was it. Still, any news is better than none, and after many years I felt cheered that a long-lost connection had at last been re-established.

In a few weeks Victorinus had settled well into the regimen of the Abbey. He was also a regular member in my classes and fluent in Latin, and I wondered whether he would be capable in due course to teach Latin to our Saxon boys.

*

A month or more passed and still I had not managed a visit to the Haven. Then I received an unexpected message. The note in Tola's bold handwriting said tersely, "Mama's seriously ill. Come at once!"

I re-read my sister's brief note and made hasty preparations. On the spur of the moment I decided to take Victorinus with me to the Haven, and by midday we stood outside our family hovel, while Pa and Tola talked urgently and quietly together.

"Last time, the herbs seemed to help," Tola was saying as we arrived. "And Mama made a recovery that's lasted a few months. Now she's very seriously ill, and nothing seems to help her."

I introduced Victorinus, explaining he had recently arrived from Rome. Pa took the lad's hand in greeting. Tola looked steadily at Victorinus for a long moment before giving him a warm hug. Looking over his shoulder, she raised a questioning eyebrow to me. I nodded. Tola knew; Victorinus was her nephew come from Rome, he would always be welcomed as such, and nothing more needed to be said.

Releasing him from her embrace, she said, "Welcome to our family, Victorinus. I also knew your mother, Paulina, when I was in Rome with my brother!"

"Wait outside, please," I said to Victorinus, and entered our family home where the hearth in the centre of the floor seemed to burn with an eternal flame.

I held Mama's hand and kissed her pale cheek.

Resting my head gently on her shoulder, I finally plucked up my courage. I knew there would be no another chance.

"Mama," I said in her ear, "I have a present for you."

She found it difficult to speak, but whispered, "A present? What present, my son?"

"From Rome, Mama. His name is Victorinus." I swallowed hard. "And he is your grandson!"

She looked at me for a long moment with rheumy eyes, trying to comprehend.

"*Your* son, Alric?"

She was so weak I could barely hear her.

"Yes, Mama. I knew his mother when I was in Rome. I did not know then that she was with my child. He was born after I came home. His mother is Paulina. She has sent Victorinus to me so he can learn to be a monk."

Wringing my hands, I said, "But Mama, he doesn't know I'm his father."

Mama's eyes closed, and for a moment I thought she had drifted away.

"Bring him," she whispered, gathering her strength. "Bring him. I want to see my grandson."

I rose carefully, wiped my eyes, composed myself and returned to the door.

"My mother wants to see you," I beckoned.

Victorinus followed me into the small hovel, blinking to adjust his eyes to the gloom, and stood by her bed. I put a hand on his shoulder and he sank to his knees.

Bending down I said, "This is Victorinus, Mama."

She slowly reached out and drew his face down to hers, looking at her grandson for several long moments, and kissed his cheek.

"Such a fine boy! I am very happy that you came."

As we rose to leave, Mama reached out and squeezed my hand.

She knew, and she understood.

*

Mama passed away soon afterwards, as though she had been waiting, waiting all this time, not knowing why, waiting for her last gift to come. She died peacefully, holding Pa's hand all through the night as her life ebbed away—not to reassure herself but to comfort Pa, the one who was left behind.

Our whole family and our neighbours at the Haven gathered for the funeral. Others walked for miles to pay their respects. Laurentius, when he received the news of Erlina's passing, insisted on preaching and conducting the funeral. I had not expected that, but it was a great relief for me to mourn with the mourners. I translated for Laurentius, adding and subtracting words and ideas as I thought best for the occasion, so that his address was well received. It seemed strange to have done something like this together.

Mama was buried in the graveyard next to the Haven, facing east, with the first cross ever to mark a grave there, driven hard into the ground. Pa was deeply distraught. The next day he marked out his own grave, right beside Mama. When he was finished, Pa turned and pointed to the plot.

"So that you all know. I go next—and I go here!"

I wiped my eyes as we walked away from the graveyard.

I had not known that grief could be so deep.

Nothing, nothing breaks the human heart so much as the loss of one's beloved.

*

Three years passed.

Victorinus grew tall, learned to speak our Saxon tongue fluently, became a budding scribe, assisted me in teaching Latin to each new class, and made friends with many of the youngsters sent by their Earls to learn the mysteries of scribing. I was proud of him, and still agonized over whether or not I should tell him that I was his father. Perhaps he guessed anyway.

Then a letter arrived for Victorinus. For the first time, he brought it to me to read on my own, while he sat down, staring out of the door. The letter was written in Paulina's hand.

"I regret to write, my beloved son, that a short while ago our dear Septimus passed away after a short illness here in Rome…"

Victorinus held back the tears as I returned the letter to him.

"I am so sorry, this must be such a devastating blow for you."

We sat together in silence for a while.

I thought of Paulina's husband, Septimus—the seventh child from a large family. What was notable was that Paulina did not refer to Septimus as 'your father', but 'my husband.' Was Paulina sending us two messages; one to Victorinus, the other to me? Would Victorinus even have noticed?

I sighed.

"Come, let us spend a quiet moment together."

Later, in November of this same year of 612, Queen Bertha passed away following a short illness. We mourned her passing as we would mourn a member of our own family. At her funeral, there was only standing room in the Cathedral, and a very large crowd waited in silence outside. The Queen had not lived to see the completion of the beloved Abbey that she had so longed for, named for *San Paolo e' Petro*. When the funeral was over, Queen Bertha was buried in the grounds, close to the Abbey.

Afterwards, Ethelbert beckoned to me to walk with him up the path to Coningsburh.

"Alric, you knew Bishop Augustinus better than anyone. What words of comfort might he have given me on a mournful day such as this?"

We continued walking. In a panic, my mind had become a complete blank. Then a few words came into my head.

"My Lord, he might have said this. 'So that you may pass through the shadows of night and come to the light of morning, take the Lord's hand. He will surely lead you.'"

*

Gisela was twenty-seven years of age in the Year of our Lord 613 when, in the summer, Gisela and King Ethelbert took their marriage vows before Archbishop Laurentius. As her closest friend, my sister Tola knew how matters had been developing, and it wasn't about romance.

Gisela had cared for Bertha's daughter Ethelburga from the time of the princess's birth, some twelve years earlier. Now, following Queen Bertha's death, the young Princess Ethelburga still needed a mother to teach her the ways of royals and help her to find a suitable royal husband. It seemed fitting that Ethelbert should wed Gisela, who would be a good and caring stepmother for young Ethelburga.

There was nothing in either the customs of our Kingdom or the

Canons of the Church to prevent the marriage—both the King and Gisela were followers of Christ, and their union was greeted with much approval.

My thoughts drifted back to Francia. Gisela was a Frankish noblewoman, now married to our King. How would King Chlothar II of Neustria view another Frankish Queen in Cantia? Would this perhaps lead to Frankish overlordship of our Kingdom?

*

That same summer, the Abbey Chapel was at last completed. Laurentius, now bearing the title of Archbishop and wearing the pallium received from Pope Bonifacius IV, consecrated the Chapel. Augustinus's remains were taken from the graveyard and placed in a sarcophagus in the north aisle, and Queen Bertha's was laid to rest in the Royal Chapel on the south aisle. Abbot Petrus's remains were also laid to rest in the Chapel.

Our ageing King Ethelbert sat solemn throughout the ceremony with Gisela, his young Queen, and Princess Ethelburga seated on either side. Bertha had wanted the Abbey even more than the Cathedral; but the Abbey was here at last, with pristine lime washed walls, dark red tiles and roof beams rising to the heavens. This was the legacy that Ethelbert and Bertha had wanted most of all.

In his funeral oration, Archbishop Laurentius made mention of King Charibertus, Bertha's father. I was glad of that, as Laurentius went on to say how much this Chapel would have meant to Charibert as a King who had no resting place in his city of Parisius, banished to the bleak hillside of Tractus Armoricani that overlooked the cold, grey sea. I knew how much having a holy place of rest like this would have meant to Bertha. Perhaps here Charibertus's own unquiet spirit would find a resting place at last.

Soon after the ceremony, Gisela asked to see me. I entered the Royal Apartments on familiar ground, and Gisela greeted me warmly. She said, "Alric, I have a letter from my father in Parisius, explaining what has happened in the Frankish kingdoms recently. King Ethelbert is now less inclined to be involved in matters from abroad these days, and has suggested I speak with you as someone he trusts."

I understood her concern, and felt pleased for her confidence in me. Wondering what this might mean, I said, "My Lady, whatever assistance I can give, I shall. What is it that concerns you?"

A shadow passed over her face as she glanced down at the letter.

"There are several issues that my father raises, and in his new position as Mayor of the Palace of Neustria, he is of course well informed."

"Say on, your Majesty," I urged.

"My father writes that an intense rivalry had developed between the two Frankish brothers, King Theudebert of Austrasia and King Theuderic of Burgundia. You know of them?"

I nodded. "I met both the young princes, with their grandmother Queen Brunhild when we passed through Cabillonum—nearly two decades ago."

"Well, the rivalry between them only served to deflect attention away from their common enemy, King Chlothar II of Neustria. On numerous occasions, the two brothers have recklessly taken up arms against each another. Recently, King Theudebert seized the region of Alsace from King Theuderic, claiming the territory for himself—but Theuderic managed to overcome his brother. Queen Brunhild then encouraged Theuderic to assassinate Theudebert, together with his son, Merovech. This made it possible for the Queen and Theuderic to focus attention on their greatest potential prize—defeating King Chlothar, and seizing the Kingdom of Neustria."

I sat back, releasing my breath.

"No, this news has not reached my ears, my Lady," I acknowledged. "Chlothar's defeat would make Theuderic the King of all Francia!"

Gisela raised a warning finger. "There is a twist in the tale, though, Alric. Princess Emma, King Chlothar's daughter—her hand in marriage had already been promised to someone!"

I was taken totally by surprise. "Promised to whom?"

"To Prince Eadbald, the King's son! This marriage would be the third generation in which a Saxon prince of the Kingdom of Cantia marries a Frankish princess. But the following year, King Theuderic of Burgundy and his grandmother the dowager Brunhild, were defeated in a battle against Chlothar. She was compelled to cede northern Neustria to Chlothar, but then immediately set about organising a fresh invasion of the Neustrian Kingdom!"

Gisela paused. "Then Theuderic also died—not on the battlefield, but of dysentery, while preparing for a new campaign against Chlothar. Brunhild apparently took desperate measures and placed her illegitimate great-grandson Sigebert II on the throne of Austrasia. The two armies met at the River Aisne, in the north of Neustria, but in a well-orchestrated act of treason, Brunhild's generals deserted her in favour of Chlothar."

"And in doing so, her generals handed Chlothar the entire realm of Francia! Ah, how shrewd! But what of Brunhild?" I asked.

"Brunhild and Sigebert fled south, the young king was killed, and the long and bloody feud between Austrasia and Neustria was ended. Chlothar was left holding the entire realm of the Franks in his hands."

I thought of the irony of all this. The one person who had no royal blood in his veins was Chlothar II, and now he was King of all Francia!

"And Brunhild? What has happened to her? Exiled in a castle or a monastery somewhere?"

"No, nothing as comfortable as that. She was taken in chains to Chlothar's hunting lodge in a forest, near to a place called the Town of the Abbots."

I remembered the lodge all too well, on an old Roman road that ran through several hamlets in the forest—the same forest that Augustinus and our companions had passed through on our way to Quentovicus. I had been aghast at how young and arrogant and foolish Chlothar was. My opinion had not changed much since then, not that my opinion carried any weight of course.

"So," Gisela concluded, "Brunhild was accused, tried and convicted of murder. Although she was a Burgundian princess, even her own Burgundian soldiers shouted for her death! They lifted her onto a camel and paraded her before the whole army, then they dragged her for miles behind a wild horse until she died."

With my head in my hands, I gave a great sigh as Gisela concluded.

"So that's how Brunhild's story has ended—bloodied and dreadful!"

"But now we come to the real purpose of this story, Alric. King Chlothar is fully aware of the advantages that a new relationship with Cantia might bring, hoping finally to extend his dominion over Ethelbert's Kingdom."

"And?"

"And as I have said, their daughter Emma will be his instrument."

Gisela paused as all this sank in, and her voice softened as she ended.

"She is only fourteen, Alric, and as inexperienced as I was at her age. What would you advise our King?"

I pondered this for a long moment.

"Perhaps you might advise the King to respond that he is grateful for the suggestion, but as Emma is not yet of age, he shall return to this proposal in due course. Also, Emma is a Christian and Eadbald, frankly, is not. For the moment, it does not seem an appropriate match. That might also postpone events for a while. But most of all, a pagan King on the throne again might severely affect the future of our mission in Cantia. The truth is, we have only just begun."

As I prepared to leave Gisela's chambers she said, "The King wanted you to know all this, Alric. You, as much as anyone, are acquainted with the main actors in Francia who have played-out this drama."

She hesitated a moment.

"I confess that I am greatly concerned about Eadbald. The King does not notice this, but his son seeks me out whenever he can. He leers at me, and makes disgusting insinuations and gestures. I can't abide having him near me! Be alert, Alric—if Emma eventually comes, keep a kindly eye on her, as you once kept an eye on me!"

XVII
LONG LIVE THE KING! CONINGSBURH

AD 616

"THIS IS OUR twentieth year after leaving Rome," Laurentius announced to his priests, "and as we are now well established, I believe we can cease using the word 'mission', and speak purely of the 'Church'."

An involuntary shudder ran through me when I heard of Laurentius's triumphant boast. I was reminded of birds dropping their prey as they opened their beaks to squawk. Our mission was far from over, and more to the point, far from well established. In reality, we were coming ever closer to a crisis. Ethelbert, our strongest supporter in Cantia, was visibly ageing, but remained a towering figure amongst many of the Saxon kingdoms. Eadbald, his immediate heir to the throne, was a pagan and determined to remain so. What chance was there that Eadbald would have a conversion—or that the Church in Cantia would even survive?

*

Mortality overtook Ethelbert in February, the Year of Our Lord 616. Ethelbert's stone sarcophagus was laid to rest in the side chapel of our Abbey, appropriately dedicated to San Martinus, set beside his first wife Queen Bertha. In so doing, we honoured the request that had meant the most to them. The funeral itself was an enormous affair, with untold numbers arriving at the Cathedral for their last farewells to an extraordinary and gifted King.

Now Eadbald's lustful eye was firmly fixed on Gisela. Not only had Eadbald inherited the Kingdom, he also desired to take his stepmother as his wife. Eadbald soon vacated his grandfather's former Royal Hall at Sturringe near Fordwic, and occupied Ethelbert's palace in Coningsburh. The new King was determined to marry Gisela, but there was an enormous impediment to Eadbald's plans. Church Law prohibited Eadbald from marrying his stepmother; such a marriage would cast Eadbald out of the Church. Also, Eadbald had offered no opposition to the Christian religion when his father was alive, but his attitude swiftly changed after Ethelbert's death.

Laurentius immediately denounced the proposed union as fornication, following the guidance Augustinus had long ago received from Pope Gregorius. In response, Eadbald's grievance against the authority of the Church grew apace, and the atmosphere between the new King and our elderly Archbishop rapidly cooled. Eadbald refused to renounce his intention to wed Gisela, and publicly declared himself a pagan, encouraging his coterie of supporters to follow him.

Determined to restore the old pagan gods and practices rejected by King Ethelbert, Eadbald and his familiars rode to the hill where Wodin's forlorn shrine still stood, making the first royal offerings in nineteen years to a pagan god.

Shortly after attending Cathedral Mass one Sunday, I accompanied Gisela and her small retinue trailing behind as we ascended the hill to Coningsburh. In the privacy of her chambers, a clearly frightened Queen confided, "Alric, as a widow, I am still in a period of mourning after King Ethelbert's passing. As a Catholic, I am appalled at the idea of marriage to a pagan! As a woman, if I may be honest, my stepson Eadbald revolts me! I must now play for time in the hope that his attentions will stray elsewhere."

It was clear to me that Eadbald was unprepared for kingship and possessed no wisdom in statecraft. As a consequence, Ethelbert's former influence was soon squandered and Gisela found herself a victim, rather than a willing bride. The example set by Ethelbert as a Christian was still shallow-rooted. A pagan marriage would undoubtedly lead to the defection of some of his Earls, who had followed Ethelbert only for the King's favour.

At an assembly of the Witan, Eadbald, now thirty-three years of age, scraped together enough votes to be acknowledged as King. He had spent most of his life occupying a dual role—as king-in-waiting for the crown, and as prince-in-pursuit of pleasure.

Queen Bertha had doted on Eadbald, her first-born, perhaps on account of his periodic fits of madness. Some said an evil spirit possessed him, vigorously shaking his body, and traditional medicines could not cure him. He was unstable and frequently given to a paralysing moodiness. Eadbald now fully rejected the Catholic Faith, having shown only token-adherence during his father's lifetime.

In only a few months, supported by a few of Cantia's Earls, a backlash against the Church gained momentum. The mood of Eadbald's followers also changed rapidly. To make matters worse, King Siebert of Lundenwic, East Saxony, died soon after his uncle, Ethelbert. Siebert's sons held common cause with Eadbald in their desire to return to pagan ways, beginning with the immediate expulsion of Bishop Mellitus from Londinium. Siebert's loutish sons led the way and Mellitus, escaping with his life, fled to Cantwaraburh from Londinium. Bishop Justus of Rofesburh soon followed, and Rofesburh's aged Earl endorsed a return to pagan worship and practices.

In April, Laurentius called a hasty meeting of his clergy and our Abbot at the Cathedral.

"Our anxiety about our safety has risen to crisis point, Alric," Abbot John confided after the meeting, "Either we stay in Cantia and face the prospect of martyrdom, or we retreat to Francia and wait for a warmer climate."

Over the next few days it became clear that Justus and Mellitus had little option but to flee across the water to Francia. Mellitus explained to a small gathering, "Given that these are the Last Days, Pope Gregorius would have said that it is more imperative to live and fight another day, than to lay down one's life in a fruitless gesture."

Laurentius rejected any suggestion of appealing to Francia for military support.

"King Chlothar has become indifferent to wider affairs of state, and everything is in the hands of the Mayor of the Palace in Parisius. His intention in this crisis is not about military aid, but tightening Francia's grip over Cantia. If the Roman Church were to be driven out, then the Frankish Bishops will be ready to fill the gap. The Franks are playing a long game, prepared to wait for a fresh opportunity to arise. They are in no hurry to give us any assistance at all."

One thing was clear to us; the future of the Church in the Kingdom of Cantia now hung on a very slender thread. I remembered Wyrd and her sisters in the heavens, weaving my future to their will. Our mission to Cantia, in what Pope Gregorius had believed was the Last Days, now seemed folly, a fraying thread set to break.

Laurentius would not be bullied into submission and waited stubbornly, with his priests, for events to become clearer. A merchant ship arrived at Fordwic, offering the opportunity of escape across the waters to Francia. The skipper carried a letter from Pope Adeodatus, the Bishop of Rome, who had also done his utmost to reverse the presence of monks in the life of the Lateran. Surprisingly, the Pope was adamantly against allowing Cantia to slide into the hands of the Franks. Laurentius was instructed to remain at the Cathedral, but in reality his Holiness in distant Rome had no idea what we were facing in Cantwaraburh.

I sent my students back to their homes, scattered throughout the Kingdom. That night, boarding the ship under cover of darkness, Mellitus and Justus quietly slipped out of Fordwic and moored overnight at Ratteburg, waiting for the dawn. In the morning the ship set sail for Quentovicus, carrying our two Bishops away to the dubious safety of the Kingdom of the Franks.

In late afternoon that same day, one of Gisela's few remaining maids arrived at the Abbey, urgently asking to see me. "My Queen requests your presence, sir. Please come at once!"

With recent events racing through my mind, I hastened up the hill to Coningsburh. Gisela's movements were now entirely restricted to the royal compound, and her stepdaughter Ethelburga had been removed from her charge.

The maid ushered me in, closing the door behind, leaving the two of us alone. This had once been Queen Bertha's quarters, now stripped of all floor coverings, wall hangings and most of the furniture, except for two uncomfortable straight-backed chairs, and a small writing desk.

I began, "My Lady, I am deeply saddened that you find yourself in such straits. However, our community at the Abbey has resolved that we will not leave, regardless of the outcome—even if the cost is high. And I believe the Archbishop has promised the same."

"Thank you, Alric." She briefly bowed her head, and looked up at me with bold determination to see this crisis through.

"You bring me much comfort. Now, let's be quick! Take a seat at the desk."

I did so, noticing some scrolls of parchment, a quill and inkwell, a candle and the Queen's wax seal, in a small earthenware tray.

"What is it that you want me to write, my Lady?"

"Firstly, a letter to my father, Count Gundoland. Can you write swiftly while I dictate? I don't know how much time we have."

I wrote as fast as I could without errors, finished the letter, and handed Gisela the pen and ink to sign in her own hand. She dripped hot wax for her seal to ensure no one else would open the letter.

Gisela had composed a moving farewell note in the event of the worst that might come to pass. She had given no secret information, writing only as a beloved daughter saying farewell to her dear father.

Gisela asked, "Have you contacts that can deliver this letter safely to my father?"

I nodded.

"Then I leave it in your hands."

I looked up from the desk. "And the second letter, your Majesty?"

I took up another parchment and wrote out what the Queen expected she would receive as her wedding dowry, and also securing the inheritance that was already hers from Ethelbert.

"Could you please keep this safely, Alric, in the event of any dispute in the future."

With both documents complete, I rose from the chair. We stood facing each other as I slid the documents deep into my pocket.

"Thank you, Alric. You don't know how much that means to me."

Gisela paused. "A date for my pagan wedding has been set—a month hence," she said bitterly. "I utterly loathe the prospect of bearing any child for Eadbald! But what can I do? To refuse would make matters far, far worse!"

"My Lady, the position you have been forced into is beyond belief! Is there no other way out of this for you?"

"You mean, other than taking my own life?" Gisela gave a mocking laugh, pulling her cloak more tightly around her shoulders.

"I am a prisoner here, Alric. I am forbidden to leave Coningsburh."

Gisela looked at me, her large eyes searching mine.

"Alric, please, may I ask of you one last request?"

"Yes, my Lady?"

"Please, Alric, please pray for me!"

*

A few days passed. I awoke in the early hours of the morning to the sound of hammering on the Abbey gate. One of Eadbald's men stood outside. "Come at once!" he commanded, "the King wants you."

I followed the messenger to Coningsburh and the King's chambers, to hear the worst possible news from a scout who had returned along the old Roman road from Rofesburh.

Eadbald said to me, "The Earl is marching on Coningsburh, ostensibly 'in support' of me as King! Now, listen to what this man has to say."

"My King," the scout stammered, "The Earl comes not only on horseback, but a large number of warriors are advancing on foot and horseback from Rofesburh—'to assist you', they say. And I have heard also that a further contingent is on its way by ship from East Saxony under command of the sons of the late King Siebert!"

"Oh? And what kind of assistance do they think we need?" Eadbald said sarcastically.

"I do not know, my Lord."

Nor did anyone else.

Eadbald growled, "Well, I have asked for none!"

The scout continued, "Combined with East Saxony's warship coming up the Temes Estuary, they put our Kingdom at considerable risk."

Eadbald became deeply agitated. "Cantia has been at peace for more than half a century. Are they now seizing the opportunity to oust me from my kingship, under the guise of offering support?"

Eadbald, widely known to have fits over which he had no control in body or mind, began to shake with the onset of another of his attacks.

I remembered Cadmon saying that after decades of peace, Cantia's military skills were no longer up to the task of war. Eadbald's reshuffle of his Personal Guard now comprised a coterie of inexperienced sycophants surrounding the King, utterly useless for any defence.

It became apparent that forestalling a rebellious mutiny would be as crucial for Eadbald as for Laurentius and our remaining clergy and monks.

"My throne will be taken from me, and Cantia made a vassal kingdom of East Saxony! An outrage! But what can we do?" he whined. "My own Guard cannot defend against the attack of seasoned warriors!"

A fear-filled silence followed as minds went numb and tongues too dry to speak. We found ourselves stepping into the void.

All eyes turned towards me.

I took a deep breath.

"There is only one option. Send for Cadmon!"

XVIII
TRAITORS' GATE

AD 616

I FOUND MYSELF galloping hard along the stony road of Waeslinga Straet to reach Ratteburg fort, two outriders accompanying me with a message for every community we passed. The command was simple. "Rally at Coningsburh by sunset in defence of the Realm!"

The road east twisted and turned around a shifting landscape, a blur of fields, forests and streams as we rode hard on our desperate mission. Halfway to Ratteburg, a small hamlet had grown around the remains of an old Roman villa. Clean water, food and a smithy were at hand. Our horses drank deeply; we waited impatiently, and then raced on to reach Ratteburg by noon. Not far from the old road and to our right, the hill dedicated to the Shrine of Wodin rose into low clouds, creating a gloomy, almost doomed atmosphere as we turned away towards Ratteburg for the last leg of our journey.

Cadmon stood watching his smithy in the workshop, re-shoeing one of the horses.

"Alric! What brings you here? Come let me give you a draught of beer. Your horse looks like you, utterly exhausted!"

"I'm here on the King's business this time, my friend! Eadbald has recalled you to your post as Captain of the King's Guard. He needs every cavalryman you can put your hands on to protect the Kingdom. Warriors are on their way from Rofesburh, and also rebels are coming from the East Saxons to seize Eadbald and usurp the Kingdom. We gather at Coningsburh before sunset!"

Cadmon's face darkened.

"Then we don't have a moment to lose. Sound the horn! I want every rider we have ready in minutes, in full armour, and on their horses!" He paused a smile briefly on his lips. "So, that idiot Eadbald has come to his senses at last!"

Earl Sighart was too infirm to participate in this venture but bustled back and forth to prepare twenty men from the stables. Tola stood in the doorway of their home with their children, and waved us farewell. We galloped out at full strength with a platoon of cavalry and onto the ancient road. At mid-afternoon we were surprised to see Coifin the pagan High Priest pass us on horseback, heading in the direction from which we had come. Cadmon hailed him, but he could have been a ghost for all the attention Coifin paid to us as he galloped on.

*

Cadmon's contingent numbered nearly forty men on horseback by the time we arrived at the heavily fortified gates of Coningsburh.

King Eadbald came out from the Royal Hall to meet us.

"Cadmon, thank the gods you've come! And with such numbers," he noted, glancing around at our horsemen.

"What news, my Lord?" Cadmon asked as he dismounted.

"The word from our scouts is that the Earl of Rofesburh is only a few hours away. King Siebert's sons have landed on the coast and are on foot, advancing through the forest—perhaps a few hours away also. What can we do, Cadmon?"

"We are not certain of their strength, either in numbers or prowess," he replied. "But to my knowledge, none have been battle-hardened for several decades, so in that respect, we are not disadvantaged, even though our numbers may be few."

Cadmon swiftly outlined his tactics, and we hastened away to position ourselves for the greatest advantage. Wooden crosses four to six feet in height were wrapped in cloth and smothered in animal fat, placed in a semi-circle around the North Gate of the town as well as our old hovels and Chapel of San Martinus, close to Coningsburh.

Night fell.

We watched and waited, hidden in the dark.

*

During the hours of darkness, another scout arrived on horseback at Coningsburh.

"My Lord!" he announced, "The Earl of Rofesburh and his warriors are approaching Coningsburh. Siebert's sons from Lundenwic disembarked at Witenstaple some hours ago. They are marching directly here!"

Another scout arrived moments later.

"They are dividing their forces, my Lord. The men from Rofesburh are skirting the old town wall on the south side to reach here. Men from East Saxony are coming up towards the town's North Gate with their torches blazing." The Abbey was the most exposed in the field below us, situated along Waeslinga Straet.

"They are preparing to make a surprise attack on the city wall," Cadmon warned, "but they are not much concerned with stealth. Well, we shall soon see what they are made of!"

We left Eadbald's compound and made our way on horseback down to one of the town gates. Saxons who had hovels in the ruins of the town milled around the bridge across the moat, their torches flaming in the night breeze, waiting for us to arrive. The gates shut behind us, and we were led through narrow streets to another wood-and-stone gate in the north wall. Cadmon and some of our cavalrymen climbed up to a platform above the gate, peering down into the darkness beyond. Pinpricks of light from burning torches began to emerge from the woods. Before they reached the narrow stream a few yards beyond the wall, our men slipped through the gate and lit fat-smeared crosses, signalling we knew where they were. The warriors from East Saxony came to a standstill and hesitated.

"Men of the East Saxons!' Cadmon's voice boomed out. "Turn back from your folly! If anyone passes between the crosses, your wives and children will never see you again! Does anyone choose to test our resolve?"

Silence.

Then a warrior stepped forward and reached the first burning cross. His armour and shield were illuminated in the flickering light as he came to the foot of the bridge. Two arrows from the wall found their mark, and with a cry the first warrior fell into the stream that ran beyond the wall. Shouts rose from the warriors and another came forward, eliciting the same outcome.

Cadmon said in a low voice to our men, "If they continue this all night, we'll be able to divide their forces and keep them away from Coningsburh. They might not succeed in breaking through to the Cathedral."

Cadmon called out to his men.

"Hold the wall! We'll see what's happening at Coningsburh!"

Cadmon leapt onto his horse. "Come, Alric!"

We crossed the silent, derelict city and burst through the Burgate on to the ancient Roman road, but all was in darkness and there were no warriors in sight. Turning to the left, we came to a well-worn pathway leading directly uphill past the Abbey, and pressed on to the Chapel of San Martinus. Above it arose the high, wooden stockade surrounding Coningsburh. Torches blazed on several poles at the main gate. Signalling to the King's warriors, we entered Eadbald's compound through a side gate and began the long wait for the men from Rofesburh to arrive.

An hour or more passed before flickering torches began to appear, glinting on helmets and spears as they steadily tramped up the road. In former days, King Ethelbert had chosen this location well;

Coningsburh overlooked everyone approaching the hill. A narrow track branched sharply up from Waeslinga Straet, passing Queen Bertha's Chapel and its small scattering of graves. The steeply sloping landscape below Coningsburh made it extremely difficult for the men from Rofesburh to mount a successful attack.

King Eadbald joined us on the wall of the fortress. The numbers from Rofesburh had swelled, but their Earl remained at the rear on his restless horse. It seemed that he had no intention of actually leading his men in an assault on the gate. Cadmon waited until the warriors below us gathered within earshot, then called out.

"Men of Rofesburh! Come beyond these crosses, and you die! Turn back now, and you live! The choice is yours. But know this. Once you attack, there will be no mercy. Are you truly willing to die for no purpose? The King does not welcome you here, arriving as a war band to seize the King's Hall. He knows your Earl's intention is not to protect the King but to seize his Kingdom! There are many of us, and you will not prevail. Turn your swords instead against the warriors of the East Saxons, who secretly plan to usurp our Kingdom and make it a vassal state. Do you wish to live as their slaves? Even as I speak, they fall one by one at the gate into Cantwaraburh. The King commands you to turn your swords against your true enemy. Now Leave. GO NOW!"

Murmuring and muttering broke out among the men from Rofesburh, their desire for battle seeping away. The King's archers stood on the barricade overlooking the Gate, their bows drawn, waiting for a command. The Earl of Rofesburh had positioned himself at the rear, his horse turning back and forth, seeming to reflect its owner's confused state of mind, while the murmur of voices below us continued.

Then a long blast sounded on a horn. The Earl of Rofesburh turned his horse in the direction of home, and with a shuffling gait, the warriors followed him home.

The rebellion, for now, was over, but the future of the Church remained gravely uncertain.

A few weeks passed. Eadbald's Kingdom had been saved, yet

the King expressed little gratitude to those among us who had done the most to keep him on his throne.

There was no change in Eadbald's attitude towards the Church. Laurentius's dire warnings of the consequences of a forced pagan marriage with a Christian bride fell on deaf ears. Eadbald proceeded to commit a sin that appalled even pagans, in that he had planned to marry his stepmother. The momentous question, whether the Christian mission should stay or leave Cantia, was rekindled once more.

*

At the height of summer, the pagan wedding uniting Eadbald and Gisela finally took place. Some of Eadbald's Earls, Thanes and cronies were in attendance. Coifin the High Priest presided over the ceremony, not in the Cathedral, but in the King's Royal Hall at Coningsburh. Eadbald, although grateful for his rescue particularly at Cadmon's hands, had shown no sign of turning away from paganism. Would there be a witch-hunt now, rounding up our Archbishop, our Abbot and our remaining priests and monks?

Days passed and the Cathedral was not boarded up, nor was any immediate attempt made to send Archbishop Laurentius and his clergy into exile. Several of our lay brothers from Rome and Turones had married local Saxon women; their families lived within the Cathedral compound. At the Abbey, Victorinus was determined that he would not leave until I did. I respected his decision, and frankly I felt glad for his support.

Not long after Gisela's marriage to Eadbald, I found myself restless and unable to sleep one night, as dire thoughts and dark images haunted my dreams. In the early hours I arose and left my small room, entering our Abbey Chapel by the north door. I glanced to my left, passing the mortal remains where San Augustinus lay enshrined. I knelt for some time, seeking some sign, some word of insight that might relieve my deep distress, certain that our lives were in mortal danger.

Then I became aware that someone else was praying in the Chapel and I arose, quietly pushing open the heavy wooden door. The Chapel was in darkness, apart from one dimly lit lamp hanging above the altar. A makeshift bed had been prepared on the floor, below the altar steps. I could scarcely make out Laurentius, lying prostrate on the floor. His cassock was pulled over his head, exposing dark whiplashes on the pale skin of his back, dimly reflected in the lamplight. There was no one else was in the Church. I stared, horrified at the sight. Laurentius's face was hidden in the folds of his cassock as he sobbed and cried out in agony.

Suddenly, he rose painfully to his feet, snatched up his cloak, and rushed out of the Chapel to Coningsburh as first light crept into the eastern sky. Pausing only a moment, I followed behind, holding up the hem of my habit as I stumbled through the damp grass. Laurentius was unaware that I was behind him as he arrived at the main gate, passing the guard without challenge, and hurried on to Eadbald's chambers. I followed only a few yards behind.

"Wake the King!" Laurentius shouted as he reached Eadbald's chambers. "I have the most urgent news for him!"

Recognising the Archbishop, the guard led the way as Laurentius hurried into Eadbald's quarters. I followed without challenge from the guards, assuming we had come together. Laurentius entered the King's chamber. I remained outside the half-closed door, attempting to peer through the crack into the gloom.

Eadbald had pulled on in his nightshirt, angered by this disturbance.

He swore and said, "Well, what is it that you see fit to wake me at this ungodly hour, Archbishop?"

"Ungodly is right, my King! Look! Look at these scars!"

Laurentius dropped the cloak from his thin shoulders and turned around to reveal the bloodstained welts across his thin, pale-skinned back.

Eadbald vomited.

"Who did this to you? Who dared to do this?" he croaked.

"No human hand has done this! All night, I have prayed for you and your Kingdom, for your people, and for Christ's sacred flock!" His face was a mask of fury, only inches from the King.

"The Apostle San Petrus came to me as I prayed, and scourged me without mercy —for *your* sake, and the sake of *your* Kingdom!"

Eadbald stood open-mouthed as he struggled to clear his mind, a great fear coming upon him as he trembled like one afflicted by the ague. He fell to his knees, unable to stand, his body shaking in the iron grip of a fit of madness.

"What am I do?" he wailed.

Laurentius, now in complete control of this unfolding drama, jabbed a finger towards Eadbald. "You must repent, or this day, you will die!" The King screamed and rolled over as one wounded and in pain.

Another jab of the finger, "And you will lose your Kingdom!" The King rolled over towards the wall, yet Laurentius had neither moved nor touched Eadbald since their encounter began.

Eadbald sobbed, "Please, I can take no more. What must I do?"

"Renounce your pagan ways! And welcome the Church to return in full strength to Cantia!"

Another jab and Eadbald found himself choking where he lay on the floor.

Laurentius pointed his finger at Eadbald one last time, and said, "Remember this! Those Earls and Princes who came here did not come to *save* you! They came to seize your Kingdom *from* you! Now where are your friends?"

The King's last cry was the longest, and the hardest, of all.

*

Archbishop Laurentius had scant compassion for Gisela's plight as a Christian, demanding that the King put Gisela away privately. Marrying his father's widow was forbidden under Church Law, yet all the blame fell on Gisela. Three months of negotiations in Coningsburh followed, led by a delegation of Franks sent from Gisela's father, including some senior members of King Chlothar's Royal Treasury, and half a dozen advocates from the City of Parisius.

Our Abbey Gatekeeper soon noticed their comings and goings between Coningsburh and the Cathedral. "All dressed like crows, come for their pickings," he snorted. Chlothar's emissaries left after several days, and returned shortly to complete the legal settlement between Gisela and Ethelbert.

Soon after this second visit, our Gatekeeper came to find me in the Scriptorium. I went out to the Abbey gate, and kissed Tola in a greeting, receiving a strong handclasp from Cadmon.

"So, today is the day," I said.

Cadmon nodded. "Our ship awaits us at Fordwic," he said, leading us up to Coningsburh. The sentry recognised Cadmon with a salute as the three of us entered the compound. Gisela had already packed her possessions into two small mule carts, and the mules and drivers accompanied us through the woods to Fordwic.

Tola and Gisela greeted each other in a tearful embrace. My sister had the gift of befriending almost anyone, from lowborn churl to the King of Coningsburh, and the friendship between these two women had grown especially strong through these recent events, culminating in Gisela's expulsion from the Royal compound.

Our small group of four set off to the port through the woods along the narrow Saxon Way.

"Truly, I could never have imagined all this would happen when I arrived here as a nursemaid for baby Ethelburga!" Gisela said.

I mentioned the comings and goings of the men from Parisius, all dressed in black, sent by King Chlothar to negotiate the settlement for Gisela's annulment.

Gisela struggled to control her anger.

"In all their time here, *no one* consulted me, and *none* of my needs were addressed. Eadbald wanted to get it all over with—in case Emma decided not to marry him after all!"

She paused and took a few deep breaths to calm herself, and said, "But I also have some good news. The midwife assured me that I am with child!"

With a shriek from Tola, we all gently hugged and congratulated Gisela.

She said, "Of course, all the blame falls on me, not on Eadbald's unsullied hands! I've been expelled from Coningsburh, never to return. But this is an exile that I joyfully embrace. You are a blessing to me, Tola," she said, as they hugged once again.

"After all this, wouldn't you rather sail out of the Wantsum and over to Francia?" I asked.

"No!" Gisela was adamant. "My father is Mayor of the Palace. My child and I would be nothing more than a pawn in his ambitions. And I cannot stay in Coningsburh because I'm an embarrassment to that grossly unattractive man! Even Archbishop Laurentius regards me as a dreadful and loose woman. As you can see, I alone have borne all this blame."

We pressed-on through the woods, leaving Coningsburh and its unhappy memories behind. Tola reached out to Gisela.

"I'm so glad you are coming to us, because we *do* want you to make your home at Ratteburg. And besides, we want to see your baby!"

"You couldn't be in better hands than Tola," Cadmon said.

"You are all so generous and kind; the only true friends I possess," Gisela said, wiping her eyes.

"But there is one happy part," she quickly brightened. "Following customary law, King Eadbald is compelled to return my dowry! And after the birth, I shall receive a large sum for the upbringing of my child. My one great regret is that Eadbald has separated me from my stepdaughter, Princess Ethelburga. We've had a very close bond since her birth. Now I'm forbidden to have any contact with her at all. She remains at Coningsburh under the guardianship of her brother until she marries, whenever that is. May God bless her, because I fear that Eadbald will not!"

After landing at Ratteburg, it did not take long to transfer Gisela's possessions to her new home, a sturdy cottage overlooking the Channel, facing towards the sea.

"Come over for a meal when you're ready!" Tola said. "There's no hurry; at your leisure."

They hugged, and as Tola, Cadmon and I walked away I asked my sister, "Do you remember, on the last part of our journey through Francia, we came across the King's hunting lodge in the woods?"

Tola nodded, "Who could forget? And that young girl who assisted me with the poor young man's wound. Why do you think of it?"

"Her name was Haldetrude. Do you remember that fellow she was with at that Lodge?"

"You mean the young, pompous King Chlothar. What of it?"

"Well, Haldetrude went on to marry that pompous young Chlothar, and one of their offspring is now seventeen years old. Her name is Emma, who is to marry King Eadbald in summer next year."

With a touch of bitterness Tola said, "Well, Emma, at least, will enjoy a Christian wedding!"

*

The following summer, Emma arrived by ship with considerable pomp, some said not unlike Queen Bertha's arrival at Ratteburg nearly four decades earlier. Laurentius performed their wedding ceremony in the Cathedral, and Emma occupied her quarters as Queen in Coningsburh.

Among the losers in all that had happened was the King's grossly ineffective and so-called Personal Guard. A weary Cadmon confided, "Eadbald has reinstated me as Captain of the Guard and dismissed his former cronies. He's sent them back to their farms in considerable disgrace. It is also noteworthy, Alric, that Derian was not present among the King's Guard on that fateful night. I think that speaks for itself."

Apart from Gisela, the Earl of Rofesburh had to shoulder the greater loss, disgraced through his futile rebellion, and stripped of his seat in the Witan. His ultimate fate was exile, and Eadbald's younger brother Ethelwald, sound in body and mind, became sub-king of Rofesburh.

*

At New Year, a letter arrived for Victorinus from the Abbess of San Quattro Coronati in Rome. Victorinus came to my study, handing me a parchment scroll. I gestured for him to sit down.

The letter began, "I regret to inform you, Victorinus, that your mother Paulina passed away after a short illness …"

I was shocked, and read the letter a few times before it sank in. I found Victorinus no less shaken than I was, as my eyes were stinging and tears flowed for the only woman I had truly loved. I looked away, struggling to compose myself. My distress may have surprised Victorinus, but I did not attempt to hide my grief. I put my arm around my son.

"My deepest sympathies, Victorinus. I truly mourn your loss, too."

He nodded, biting his lip, too overwhelmed to speak.

"Do you want to return home?" I asked after a long pause.

Victorinus shook his head. "No, I have no desire to return to Rome. My life is here now. After all we've been through, this is certainly my home."

Soon afterwards news came of my father's death also. Everything seemed out of joint these last few years, with so much tragedy and gloom. I returned to Sandwic Haven with Victorinus for the sad business of burying my beloved Pa. Everyone in the Haven turned out. I took the funeral and spoke of Pa's fortitude and faithfulness, and his care for his four children and our families. After prayers for the departed, and together with Godric and Victorinus, we laid out

Pa in a linen cloth, dug a grave next to Ma as we had promised, and fashioned a wooden cross, hammering it deep into the soft earth.

Afterwards, we sat together over a pot of broth and reminisced about his life.

"It's people like Pa who keep the world turning," I said. "Unassuming, loving, thoughtful, skilled—you name it, he lived it."

As the time came for us to return to the Abbey, my younger brother Godric touched my sleeve.

"I suppose, you think of yourself as head of the family now."

"Yes," I said firmly, acknowledging my responsibility now as the oldest in our family; and for the first time ever, Godric and I reached out to each other in a warm and tearful embrace.

XIX
LAURENTIUS

Ratteburg, AD 619

A TIME OF consolidation now brought this stage of our mission to an end. There was little growth to show for it, and yet the needs of our two institutions, the Abbey and the Cathedral, absorbed more and more of almost everyone's time and energy. Meanwhile, I tried to cope with my own family's grief.

Then, in February of 619, Archbishop Laurentius died.

The funeral for Laurentius took place in the Cathedral, and afterwards he was buried at the Abbey. A large number of mourners came for his last farewell, surrounded by clouds of incense, chants and prayers. He deserved every moment of it. At the foot of the cross, I laid everything that had given me cause for resentment and criticism in the course of his ministry.

At the last, after everything we attempted had failed to keep Eadbald safe and on a steady course, it was Laurentius who, metaphorically, stood alone on the bridge bellowing, "You shall not cross over!" And Eadbald did not pass.

As Laurentius's body was laid to rest, I reflected that the most unlikely people might be the ones through whom the course of history changes. Laurentius was always a difficult man to work with, and a strange choice for the mission, but ultimately he was the instrument of King Eadbald's conversion with a significant influence in restoring Pope Gregorius's mission to the Kingdom of Cantia.

Mellitus was the obvious successor, and became Archbishop in his place.

*

My grief was compounded that year by the most significant event at Ratteburg—the passing of Earl Sighart, said by all to be the most honest, competent and trustworthy man in the entire Kingdom. He was deeply mourned by his devoted wife, Odelinda, and all who knew him. The funeral was attended by vast numbers of people, including the monks and priests who had known the Earl since we first arrived from Rome.

Derian was not told of Sighart's passing, nor was he invited to his father's funeral. He had not been seen at Ratteburg for many years, and rumour had it he was living with a coven of witches at Wodin's Shrine. The two brothers, Cadmon and Derian, could not be more different from each other, as I observed Cadmon step into his new role as Earl.

The family invited me to stay for a while after the funeral, which I was glad to do.

The following day a stranger arrived at Ratteburg, asking for Cadmon.

"I bring a message from your brother Derian," the rider said.

"I do not have a brother," Cadmon snapped, but the messenger continued.

"He says that now your father has died, he wants his share of the estate."

Cadmon stared at the messenger in amazement. His cheeks reddening with rage, Cadmon stepped forward, seizing the horse's reins.

"You dare to come here, trespassing on my estate, to deliver a message without any condolences to my mother on the death of her husband! You tell me that Derian has the gall to demand half of the estate, when he has long since been excluded from any benefit arising from my father's passing!"

The rider replied uneasily, "I am only the messenger, sir."

"Then tell him I shall meet with him at Wodin's Shrine tomorrow, and settle matters with him once and for all!"

The messenger departed and Cadmon's face darkened at the prospect of the forthcoming meeting.

"I'll go with you," I volunteered, and Cadmon nodded. Odelinda was distraught and Tola was furious when Cadmon broke the news to them.

"What if they attack you?" Tola challenged.

"I'll take some of my men with me. We'll be alright," Cadmon replied grimly.

*

On the morrow we rode out across the bridge to the mainland, following an overgrown Roman road towards Estringe. Cadmon's jaw was set like stone as he led the way, riding in silence. The atmosphere was distinctly gloomy, the air chilly. From a distance I could see the outline of Wodin's Shrine on top of the only hill in the surrounding area, partially hidden by grey gloomy cloud that never seemed to allow sunshine to penetrate. In the distance, wisps of smoke rose above tall trees surrounding the hill. By late morning we approached a coven of thatched dwellings arranged in a circle, facing an open stretch of level ground perhaps fifty yards or so below the Shrine of Woden. Smoke drifted from a few fires, and dogs barked as we approached.

Strange, I thought with a shudder, not a child in sight. The water in a well a few yards away was so dark I could see no reflection, and a disgusting stench rose from its depths. Two men were hard at work in the yard. A fire blazed in the centre of the clearing, throwing up black smoke as we approached.

Everyone stopped working as we approached, staring at us, but saying nothing. Despite the growing warmth of the day, a cold shiver ran through me. Were they merely fearful because of the sudden arrival of our horsemen? Or was something more sinister in play?

The wind rustled the leaves; among the trees I spied the foliage and flowers of hemlock and berries of deadly nightshade, knowledge Tola had shared with me over the years. At that moment a woman, dressed entirely in black from her headscarf to her shoes, appeared in the doorway of her hovel. It was difficult to guess her age. Her self-confidence and the way she carried herself suggested she might be High Priestess of Wodin's Shrine. Behind her in the gloom, I caught a glimpse of a large figure shuffling towards the door of the woman's hovel, his features hidden beneath a thick beard. Derian was scarcely recognisable. Cadmon did not dismount; he stared at Derian, and the tension grew. Then in a cold voice, he addressed his brother directly.

"Tell me what it is that you ask of me."

Derian spoke slowly, his words slurred, and I could understand why he had not come to Ratteburg personally. What I saw left me appalled; it had been beyond Derian to speak or think coherently for himself. He looked at the woman; she raised her eyebrows and nodded.

"I want my share of my father's estate," he said in a blurred drawl. It was obvious that Derian was not the initiator of this request.

Cadmon said, "My father made his wishes quite plain. You forfeited your rights long ago. The Eastringe Estate has been settled, and Ratteburg is in my hands."

"Come now, come now," the woman interrupted; "let us share this cup of peace together." The witch brought forth a beautiful goblet, crafted from gold and inset with a precious jewel. "Here," she said in a consoling tone, offering the cup to Cadmon.

"After you," he waved his hand.

"That is not our way," said the witch. "The person of highest honour must drink first. Surely, you are not frightened? Are you a coward? Will your god not protect you?"

Something was stirring in Derian. Perhaps, for the first time, he needed to face his younger brother who now held a higher status than he.

"You always were a coward," he slurred and spat, attempting to square up to Cadmon. "Running to father at the slightest upset."

Derian grabbed the goblet from the witch, and with his eyes fixed on Cadmon, he drank. "No!" she screamed.

"You see," he began, laughing at Cadmon. "You are the coward!"

But the laugh died on his face as he grasped at his throat, dropping the goblet.

I stared aghast as the drama unfolded. The dogs began barking, running to and fro, bewildered and frightened; but in the midst of all this chaos, only one thing was certain—Derian had breathed his last.

"He no longer serves my purposes," the witch sneered in contempt. "He promised so much; lands, wealth..." She tailed off, turning to Cadmon. "But you! You show *so* much more promise!"

Cadmon recoiled in disgust.

"Wrap him in a shroud," he ordered, looking to the men of the coven. "Bury him up at the shrine. As for the rest, you have an hour to pack your possessions and leave this place. *Go!* Do it now!"

Afterwards the site was deserted, and eerily quiet. Even the birdsongs had ceased. Cadmon took a torch, lit it from an open fire, and ignited each of the hovels. We watched as the roofs caved in and the wooden walls caught fire, until only smouldering embers remained. As Cadmon turned away, something flat, circular, and shining caught his eye. Carefully scooping it up, he held it out for me to see, like a large flat coin, with a jewel set in it.

"It reminds me of your coin, Alric. Here, take it."

I shook my head. "No, I don't think so, Cadmon; I believe this one is yours."

The two of us walked up to Wodin's Shrine, where the men had dug a grave for Derian. Cadmon thrust the flaming torch into the shrine at several places, and we stood back and watched as smoke billowed and flames reduced it to ashes.

Afterwards, we threw sand over the dying embers.

Cadmon turned to me and said, "This will be a good place to build a chapel one day."

On our return along Waeslinga Straet, at a sharp bend, we turned east towards Ratteburg. The day was hot, and the clouds that hung above Wodin's Shrine had drifted away.

Not many days later, Cadmon took his place as the Earl of Ratteburg in the Assembly of the Witan. Odelinda could not long survive the passing of her beloved husband, and within the year she followed Sighart to the grave.

For my part, I became absorbed again in teaching reading and writing for new recruits, drawn from all eight Earldoms of Cantia. In spite of all our activity at the Abbey, it remained the case that we were not growing in our mission. The dust of death had begun to settle on the Abbey, on my desk, and on me; and the winds of change were too weary to blow.

Then unexpectedly, a long way from the Kingdom of Cantia, and through a mere handful of people, one fatal event forever changed the purpose of our mission.

*

In the spring of the year 625, on the hill at Coningsburh, Princess Ethelburga celebrated her twenty-fourth birthday. Below the hill, changes at the Abbey passed almost unnoticed until, at the end of breakfast, Abbot Ruffinian rose from his chair and reached for a small bell, resting on the table.

"I wish to announce," our Abbot began, "that I bring news of great joy today. You will be pleased to know that Princess Ethelburga has agreed to give her hand in marriage to Edwin, King of Northumbria!"

Spoons and forks hammered out approval on the heavy wooden tabletops. Something that brought Cantia into the wider world of

Kingdoms was beginning at last, and we all greeted the announcement with great enthusiasm.

King Edwin, an ally of Eadbald our King, was thirty-nine years of age, a widower, and the most powerful King in all the land. Bits and pieces of Edwin's story swiftly circulated. He had been in exile in his youth, fleeing for his life from King Ethelfrith of Northumbria. He once had a price on his head, and for several years he had taken refuge in King Raedwald's Court; and later he had overcome his archrival, King Ethelfrith, to take the Throne of Northumbria. The most interesting news for us was the rumour that, while in exile in the Court of King Raedwald, Edwin was visited in a vision by Paulinus our priest, who had come to Cantia with the second wave of the Cantwaraburh mission. In this vision Paulinus is said to have exhorted Edwin to embrace the Christian faith, and the wheels for a new dispensation began to turn in a new direction at last.

Soon after Edwin's proposal to Ethelburga, Paulinus was consecrated Bishop of Eoforwic and appointed to accompany Princess Ethelburga on her voyage to Northumbria, In July, a ship was prepared for the bride's journey to Eoforwic, where Edwin awaited his bride-to-be. Ethelburga was highly intelligent and educated, caring and upright, able to provide a stable and secure royal household for Edwin, something that Edwin the widower needed most.

Forbidden by Eadbald ever to have contact with Gisela again, she heard of the journey that Ethelburga was about to undertake, realising this might be her last chance ever to see Ethelburga again. On the day of departure, Gisela waited for hours on the ancient walls of Ratteburg for the ship to pass by, holding aloft her distinctive scarlet cloak on a pole, waiving to the ship as it passed by Ratteburg on its way to the open sea.

Afterwards, Gisela joined Tola on the cliff with everyone else from the estate.

"I saw her," she cried triumphantly. "This is my step-daughter's last farewell! I saw her, and waved to her until my arms ached! And I know Ethelburga saw me too. We strengthened each other for whatever lies ahead. "

XX
STIRRINGS IN THE NORTH

AD 633

A PERIOD OF relative calm followed. Years went by, and I continued to live a contented life, giving thanks constantly for the companionship of my son. Long before my mother Erlina's death, Victorinus had already become an unspoken part of our family. In the Abbey I was kept busy teaching, but once again, we found ourselves drawn into a time of unrest.

A new development occurred, beginning with a summons to King Eadbald's private chambers.

I knocked and peered around the door.

Eadbald sat at a table covered with a large pile of unopened correspondence. He was overweight as ever, with heavy jowls and pallid skin, looking much older than his almost three score years.

"Enter!" the King growled. I bowed and stood a few feet from his table, with no idea why he had summoned me.

"You still teach grammar and writing, don't you? This came yesterday, from my sister Ethelburga, carried by a messenger who cannot read. Nor can I. She seldom corresponds, but Spelboda, her emissary, assures me this matter is most urgent."

He picked up the parchment, seal unbroken, and handed it to me.

"Read it, and tell me what she says."

"My Lord," I said with a low bow, and using my belt knife carefully eased-open the seal. Queen Ethelburga had written in Latin on a single sheet of parchment. I read the letter through, and began to read aloud.

"My Lord, I know you are aware that my husband, King Edwin, has received baptism and now speaks freely to all his Earls and Thanes concerning matters spiritual. It is in this spirit that he called together his warriors to wage war on the brutal King Penda of Mercia, and bring his wicked ways to heel.

Yet my dreams are deeply troubled of late, and ghostly messengers whisper constantly in my ear that the outcome will not turn out as we would wish. I have begged Edwin to delay this battle until next spring, but to no avail.

For this reason, I must now take all precautions lest the outcome is unfavourable. I therefore beseech you to send a warship to the River Ure without delay.

I shall also commandeer a merchant ship to take my family, my retainers, and myself to an island where the waters of two rivers flow into the Humbre Estuary. Should the King's battle be lost, and he falls by the sword (may God forbid), the island I have mentioned is where we shall await your warriors and their ship to make our escape.

With gratitude and earnest prayers,

Your sister,

Ethelburga."

I looked up.

"The Queen has also added a PostScript. She writes, *'Please, I beg of you, send a ship in all haste!'*"

Eadbald rose heavily from his chair and paced back and forth, coming to an unusually swift decision.

"Send for Adelmar!"

Adelmar, Captain of the King's Guard was married to Erlina— Tola and Cadmon's daughter. Adelmar soon appeared, and I stood aside as the two men attended to details—a skipper for a fast ship, a full crew of warriors, weapons and food supplies.

Adelmar concluded, "My Lord, I would also suggest Cadmon accompany us. He is the most experienced warrior in your Kingdom. The tactics, if necessary, should be placed in his hands."

To my great relief, and for once, no one suggested my name.

*

On a balmy day at the end of September AD 633, with the warmth of summer still upon us, I sat outside the Mead Hall at Ratteburg with Tola and Cadmon, Erlina their daughter, and her husband Adelmar, discussing Queen Ethelburga's plea. Queen Ethelburga's emissary Spelboda sat with us, nervous and anxious that they be on their way without delay.

Tola was furious.

Glaring at Cadmon, she said, "You promised me no more of your adventures away from home! And now you want to involve yourself in another battle? You are breaking your vow to me, and risking your life again. I don't wish to be a widow before my time, Cadmon."

"I'm not going to war," Cadmon argued. "The King's letter from his sister is clear. Eadbald wants me to ensure his sister's safety—and her children's. I'll be nowhere near the battlefront."

"But why you? Eadbald could send anyone from his Guard!"

"He is!" Cadmon countered triumphantly. "Adelmar will lead us."

Tola turned from red anger to pale.

"Not only my husband but my son-in-law as well?" she rebuked.

Cadmon spoke in a conciliatory tone, "Look, the King wants to offer Edwin and Ethelburga the best support we can give."

"Why must he involve you? You're too old to get involved in someone else's battles!"

"He is not asking me to be involved, except for their safety in bringing them back home, should that be necessary. No battle, no fighting."

Tola glared at Cadmon, far from convinced.

"So, I'm not breaking my promise, Tola; this is a mission of mercy. I'll make you this oath. I won't become involved in King Edwin's war, only the safety of the Queen and her children."

My niece Erlina agreed. She said to Adelmar, "Yes, my thoughts entirely! I know you'll all take care to stay out of trouble!"

*

Weeks passed before the ship returned to Ratteburg. Everyone on the estate seemed to have turned out to welcome them home as the ship came alongside the jetty. Tola and Erlina stood on the grassy slope, anxiously looking for a glimpse of Cadmon and Adelmar. I slipped away, running down to the jetty, pushing my way through passengers and crew as they began to disembark. Cadmon stood in the prow, supervising a shrouded body carried off the ship.

"Who is that?" I asked one of the crew.

"Adelmar," he said. I swung round to look back at the grassy knoll. My eyes found Erlina's, and I pushed my way back to reach her. Erlina shook her head, her shock, disbelief and grief overwhelming her. I threw my arms around her as she sobbed, her whole body now trembling.

"No!" she wailed, and we clung to each other, both of us shedding our tears. Tola put her arm around Erlina's shoulder.

"What happened Alric? For the love of God, tell us what happened!"

Erlina sobbed, "He wasn't meant to die, Ma! He promised me!"

The body was brought up the slope on a stretcher and laid on the grass. Erlina trembled as she drew back the shroud and looked at her husband's face, and wept into her kerchief. As she clung to

Adelmar, my gaze turned briefly to Tola's herb patch, a short distance beyond the Mead Hall. I shook my head, and looked away.

There is no balm for a grief such as this.

Queen Ethelburga had now also disembarked. Gisela, once her nursemaid, then her tutor, finally her companion and stepmother, came forward to greet the Queen. The two women tearfully embraced; they had not seen each other for eight years.

"As one Queen to another, come and see me soon," Ethelburga said as she prepared to leave. "I shall be at Coningsburh."

Gisela shook her head.

"Both my daughter Mildred and I are still banished from coming anywhere near to Cantwaraburh—on your brother's orders, alas."

"Then I will come to you," Ethelburga responded.

"One day, perhaps. We shall see."

They embraced again, and the royal entourage returned to the ship for the last miles to Fordwic.

At Adelmar's funeral at Ratteburg, Cadmon spoke words of praise for his son-in-law, and words of encouragement for their widowed daughter. He ended saying, "Our world is full of danger, and much darkness occupies the hearts of men. Yet although we are downcast now, great grief will be overcome by a greater love. We must search for the good in this world so that the dark deeds of evil men may never triumph."

After Adelmar's burial, our families sat outside the Mead Hall. Erlina sat with her head bowed and covered. Tola put her arm around her daughter, and Cadmon rose to tell Adelmar's story.

*

Cadmon said, "After three days out at sea, our ship anchored in the shelter of a small island, near the north bank of the Humbre Estuary. There was no sign of Queen Ethelburga, and local fishermen assured us that no ship had anchored there in the last week.

Queen Ethelburga's emissary, Spelboda, together with Adelmar and me, rowed across to the mouth of the Trisentona River. The banks narrowed the more we ventured upstream, until at a small fishing village called Adelingesfluet, we secured the services of a ferryman to take our small party through the marshes. We entered the watery Kingdom of the Isle of Axholme, and the ferryman led us to the King's Hall.

King Hussa informed us that we had arrived too late; a battle had already taken place two days earlier on a hill, some miles away to the west at a place called Haethfelth. Penda of Mercia was a shrewd predator, bent on destroying Northumbria, and had joined forces with King Cadwallon of Gwynedd. Together they led a combined army of ten thousand Britons and many Mercian Saxons in an effort to destroy Edwin, who was now hopelessly outnumbered, tricked and ambushed. Edwin and his men were trapped with their backs to the River Poulter. There was no bridge to cross, and no escape left for Edwin. Two thousand of his warriors perished that day as he fought and died alongside his older son, Osfrid.

King Hussa led me and our companions across the yard to Edwin's body, wrapped in a linen shroud and placed in front of an altar to Wodin. The sight was sickening—the body was headless: after the battle, Cadwallon had thrown Edwin's severed head into a sack, and rode north at once to capture Edwin's Queen at Eoforwic. While the victors were still in a frenzy of stripping the bodies, two of Edwin's warriors secretly brought Edwin's body to King Hussa at Belwode, and then melted away to Northumbria.

Adelmar was both deeply moved and greatly troubled, and wanted to give King Edwin a proper burial. Hussa reckoned that if we departed for the Forest before dawn, our party would arrive at a suitable burial place by noon. It was a secret place, but it meant riding ever deeper into the forest—and further into Penda's territory.

Hussa and Adelmar strapped King Edwin's body to one of the horses and we rode south, into Mercia's Great Forest, ever deeper beneath a broad, oak canopy. We arrived after two hours at an enormous oak tree above a shrine, dedicated to Thor. The four of us swiftly dug out a shallow resting-place in the earth floor of the wooden building, and lowered King Edwin into his grave. Hussa named the place 'Edwinstowe,' scattering fallen leaves over the grave to hide it before we set off again through the forest.

As we four riders returned over a patch of open heath, we became aware of mounted riders galloping furiously behind us, attempting to overtake us.

"Penda's men!" Adelmar shouted, and I swung round to engage two of the horsemen. They went down almost at once. My spear found the third, and the rider fell from his horse. The last warrior retreated towards a low hill, turning only once to release his arrow, as King Hussa galloped furiously to overtake him. Without his shield guarding his back, Adelmar had no defence against that arrow. He swayed and fell forward on the horse's neck. I drew alongside Adelmar, examined his wound and urged him to hold on, offering words of encouragement, and a promise we would be back on the ship soon. King Hussa, his sword streaked with blood, assured our party that none of Penda's men were left alive. Edwin's grave would remain undisturbed and the secret of his burial-place kept safe.

Later, after hasty farewells to King Hussa, the boatman pushed away from the landing-place and thrust strongly through the reeds to join up with the Trisentona River. Blue sky gave way to dark clouds blotting out the sun. Gloom descended, and a strange evil seemed to shadow us. Adelmar's breathing came with increasing difficulty. We rowed our small boat back from Adelingesfluet, across the estuary to the ship waiting at the island. It was dusk when our party returned; one last cough came from Adelmar's throat, and he breathed his last.

Many hands carefully lifted Adelmar's lifeless body onto the deck. He was wrapped in a shroud and laid carefully in the prow of the ship. All the while the crew stood like statues, looking on in silent respect, deeply mourning our Captain.

At first light the following morning a merchant ship came into sight. Queen Ethelburga with her children, Bishop Paulinus and other members of her retinue, had all escaped, making the journey south from Eoforwic to join our waiting ship. With everyone on board we set sail at once, and returned Adelmar to his home here in

Ratteburg; and Queen Ethelburga and her children were all saved from certain death."

*

Erlina wept as her father ended his account of events, not only for Adelmar, but also for her mother and also Queen Ethelburga.

Tola reached out and rested her hand on Cadmon's shoulder as she whispered, "I'm so grateful you went with him, Cadmon. You did the right thing."

Cadmon had spoken clearly and well, like a bard, telling the tale of a great warrior. I knew too, that Adelmar's last journey would be told and retold countless times in years to come and in the same manner, with his memory celebrated to the end of this age.

XXI
A GENERATION RISING

633-635 *AD*

DOWAGER QUEEN ETHELBURGA took up residence in Coningsburh at the invitation of her brother, King Eadbald, together with her children and ladies in waiting from Northumbria. If I had expected Ethelburga to withdraw for a period of mourning, I was greatly mistaken. A few days after Ethelburga's arrival at Coningsburh, one of her ladies arrived at the Abbey.

"My name is Hild," she said. "I bring you a note from my Queen."

I was intrigued as I read Ethelburga's invitation to meet in her chambers at Coningsburh, and discuss future plans for a monastery.

"I would be delighted!" I responded; "I shall meet with her tomorrow afternoon as requested."

Hild thanked me, remaining seated and composed, looking at me with an unwavering gaze.

"My Queen informs me that you came here from Rome, together with your late Archbishop Augustinus, even though you are a Saxon by birth?"

I nodded. "That is so."

"I have heard something of your story. I am curious to know how you came to be in Rome, and no less, how you were able to return. Could you tell me how you came to meet Pope Gregorius?"

The impression Hild left on me was indelible. Her father was a nephew of King Edwin, and Hild was of the Royal Household of Deira. She was tall and severe in appearance, not unattractive, with an inscrutable expression, neither friendly nor unfriendly. I took a deep breath, and began to tell her everything; everything, that is, except about Paulina and our son, which is the hidden heart of my story.

"Thank you, Alric" Hild responded when I had come to the end. "I shall remember your acount, which is rightfully a legend. I shall ensure that it is scribed as part of the record I keep of Pope Gregorius's mission that he sent here to Cantia."

After a moment's hesitation, she revealed something of her own intentions.

"I find myself increasingly called to the monastic life. One day I hope to return and establish an abbey in Northumbria, somewhere on the coast perhaps. In the meantime, may God be with us in all in what we are about to undertake."

Afterwards I sat for some time, staring at nothing in particular, reflecting on my life as I had recounted it, and on Ethelburga's and now Hild's interest in monasteries. The call to monastic life seemed to be gathering momentum, but apart from our Abbey, nothing else was planned at Cantwaraburh. Attention was beginning to be drawn towards more remote places, far removed from Cantwaraburh.

Victorinus came to my study, looking for one of the works of Aristotle brought from Rome several years earlier. I raised my head as he entered.

"You have a very thoughtful look, Grammaticus!" Victorinus said. "Anything on your mind?"

I told Victorinus of my encounter with Hild, and her desire to found a monastery in her homeland of Northumbria, at some future time.

"What are your thoughts?" I asked.

Victorinus sat tapping softly on the leather cover of the volume he had selected, his brow furrowed.

"I don't think I have the calling for what she has described," he confided. "Our Archbishop Honorius is a good man, the Cathedral is well organised, the King and his Earls come here frequently for the festivals and ceremonies. I wouldn't consider all that as a failure."

All the same, my own sense was that something new was stirring, but I wasn't clear what it might be.

*

Ethelburga scoured the coast for a suitable place for her Abbey, to include both men and women under her oversight as Abbess. Lyminge, just four miles inland from the coastal fishing village of Folcstan, was chosen as the site—and a long way from Eadbald's Royal Hall at Coningsburh.

King Eadbald was generous with his support, although Ethelburga had considerable resources of her own, so that her plans were soon taken in hand. She drew together several postulants, both men and women, willing to consider a monastic life. In preparation, I trained several at our Priory of San Martinus, teaching how to read and write, memorise the daily Offices and portions of the Scriptures, as well as how to use herbs and remedies for the sick.

Two years later, in spring of AD 635, I made the journey to Lyminge for the formal dedication of the Abbey.

"The site is perfect, Alric," Ethelburga enthused as she showed me around the grounds on the day before the Archbishop's dedication. In addition to the Chapel, there were numerous buildings to provide accommodation, laundry facilities, a refectory and a library. We left the Abbey grounds, and walked a short distance away to the King's Royal Hall near to the King's Royal Compound.

"My father King Ethelbert rebuilt this Hall in the year that I was born, so this was always a special place for me," Ethelburga said. "My mother and father brought me here every year, during their annual progress around the Kingdom."

On the following morning Archbishop Honorius dedicated the Chapel, installed Ethelburga as Abbess, and blessed all the postulants as well as the Abbey grounds. I breathed a sigh of relief—the first dual monastic foundation in these Isles was established at last.

XXII

A BIRTHDAY CELEBRATION

May, AD 639

IN THE MONTH of May in the year 639, I turned sixty years of age. Tola and Cadmon invited me to Ratteburg to mark the occasion. A soft and warm breeze wafted across the estuary as Victorinus sprang on to the quay steadying the boat, and we climbed up the grassy knoll to the Mead Hall. Two, perhaps three score family, friends and well-wishers called out their greetings as we approached.

"Thank you! Thank you! What a surprise! And so many people here!" I exclaimed, surrounded by young and old, friends and family.

My two sisters Tola and Greta greeted me, Tola the first to hug and plant a kiss my cheek.

"Thank you, my dear sister for this gift! I wasn't expecting anything like this!"

Earl Cadmon gripped my hand in traditional salute.

"At sixty, Alric, you are now twenty years beyond your expected lifespan! Well done!"

Inside the Mead Hall, wicker baskets full of food from the estate, oven-baked bread, and abundance from the ocean awaited us. Cadmon rapped the table, gave a brief welcoming speech, and the feast began. Tola, in a long white linen dress and a dark blue scarf, with

Cadmon in a leather jerkin and hose, circulated around the Hall, topping up beers and mead. Cadmon was still a handsome, vigorous figure, and they made a beautiful couple.

Conversation within the Mead Hall flowed on through the afternoon, fuelled with vast amounts of food and drink. Cadmon and Tola worked their way around opposite sides of the hall, greeting, chatting, laughing, putting everyone at ease, as Cadmon's parents Odelinda and Sighart had done in years gone by. Tola's once midnight-dark hair was turning grey, but still, she walked tall and upright, refusing to bow to the burden of age.

"You are still beautiful," I held Tola's hand. "It must be your miracle herbs!"

"I'll give you some later, Alric. They'll take years off you. I can see you need it!"

I laughed.

"Tell me, sister, is Erlina still intent on joining the Lyminge monastery?"

Tola sat down, a shadow passing over her face. "I regret to say the answer is yes. Still, I can understand how she feels. And she seems genuinely keen to become a postulant. Much as I would miss her, I shan't stand in her way, Alric."

Cadmon joined us and filled my tumbler.

"How is our warrior doing?" I asked. "Almost didn't recognise you without your cavalry outfit!"

"Well, all I ever wanted to be was a warrior, as you well know."

"And so you are!"

Cadmon shook his head in a weary gesture of despair. I cupped my ear to hear above the rising noise. Cadmon put down the jug of beer and leaned closer across the table.

"Our Kingdom is full of meat-heads, Alric. Their backsides burn for war and hearts lust for wealth, competing for the King's praise! They want bards to sing songs after they are gone, making themselves immortal. But the true warrior does not think about himself. His aggression is always disciplined, taught in the arts of battle with the weapons of war. He does not seek glory; that is for others to proclaim. Does not your Good Book say that power and authority are rooted in suffering for the sake of others?"

Behind me, someone touched my sleeve.

"Remember me?"

I turned to see Gisela, flaxen-haired, her cheeks glowing, skin as clear as ever. She gave me a bright smile and we sat chatting together. After a while she fell silent, looking distracted as she sipped her mead. I said nothing, waiting for her to continue.

"I worry constantly about Mildred," she confided at last. "I know she is in no danger at Lyminge, but it's not her wish to remain there forever. But Eadbald is adamant. I wish there was a way to bring her home, Alric; really I do."

We said no more on the matter, but my mind continued to ponder; was there even the smallest possibility of bringing Mildred home again?

Cadmon broke into my thoughts. "Drink up," he urged, pouring from his flagon, "there's more to come before the night is over!"

*

Much later into the night, when most of our family and guests had drifted off home and only half a dozen of us still remained, the tallow candles flickering and illuminating our faces, we sat together around the high table where Sighart and Odelinda had always sat, and we began to reminisce about many things that had led us to this moment in our lives.

"Tell us your life story, Alric!" Cadmon challenged.

I laughed. "That would be too tedious; but now that you've asked…"

Everyone groaned theatrically.

"Today I am sixty years old. At each stage of my life I could never have foreseen the changes that each decade would bring. At the age of ten, for example, when my life changed so dramatically…"

Cadmon interrupted, "You and I were doing the same thing, Alric, standing in the slave market in Rome, waiting for someone to buy us. I remember it well!"

"Yes, and during those years in Rome, I could not have imagined the life I would later lead in Cantwaraburh!"

Cadmon mused, "I have often wondered, what would have happened to us if that slaver, Felix, had not been able to find the Haven in the thick mist on that fateful morning, when he came looking for me? How would your life have been different if this had never happened? Would you have been content? Come, Alric, tell us what would have been different?"

I sat back and blew out my cheeks.

"I suppose I would have continued as a fisherman, like Pa. But in Rome, I—we—entered another world, learning another language and how to write and read, and gaining some insight into the politics of the powerful families ruling that city. What about you, Tola?"

She smiled. "Well, that first year I served as a chamber maid to Bertha's mother, Queen Ingoberga. I missed Ma and Pa dreadfully, and I was desperate for them to know I was alive and well. In some ways, I suppose it was much harder for Ma and Pa than it was for me. But Queen Bertha's mother was very good to me, and after she died, when I was in the convent in Massilia during those six years, I learned a great deal. Then you and Cadmon came and found me!"

Cadmon turned to me. "So in Rome, Alric, what if the Pope had not decided to launch his mission to Cantia, and we had remained in Rome instead?"

"Then my nagging concern for Ma and Pa and the family would never have been put to rest, like an open wound that never heals."

I thought of Paulina, and how matters could have turned out differently for us; but with Victorinus at the table, I said no more. Instead, my thoughts turned to our long-deceased Archbishop Augustinus.

"I was deeply indebted to Augustinus for his friendship, his determination, and his wisdom. His legacy lives on. But, if I had heard that some disaster had swept all our family away at the Haven, I would have remained in Rome; and because I didn't know what had happened to Ma and Pa in all those years, it left me with a never-ending ache to come home. Besides all this, I had made a promise to find you, Tola."

My eyes began to sting with tears. "It was the last thing I remember, calling out to you as Felix dragged you away to the slave market in Francia."

Tola put her arms around me as we wept together.

"But you did find me," she said, sitting back and wiping her eyes. She reached out to Cadmon.

"You both did! Finding me in Massilia gave back almost everything I had lost."

My life had been punctuated by so many unexpected events. I wondered if my remaining years, however long they were granted to me, would now follow a more predictable course?

XXIII
RETURN TO LYMINGE

Autumn, AD 639

TOWARDS THE END of the year, Erlina finally resolved to enter the Abbey at Lyminge. Cadmon and Tola were willing to support their daughter, and now six years after her husband Adelmar's death, we boarded Cadmon's ship at Ratteburg.

I also had a particular reason for visiting the Abbey at Lyminge again. Mildred had not seen her mother Gisela for four years. King Eadbald's fall from grace had been too great to allow the daughter born to him and Gisela ever to return to the Royal Court. This unfortunate child was the King's deepest embarrassment and Eadbald wanted her hidden away. From the day that Lyminge Abbey was consecrated, the King had insisted that Mildred be shut away in the Abbey, out of sight and out of mind.

My task was simple: to speak to the Abbess on Gisela's behalf, release her daughter Mildred from the Abbey, and bring her home to Ratteburg. I set off with no expectation that what Gisela wanted most could be achieved.

Tola, Erlina, Cadmon and I sailed down the coast past the fort at Dubris, and continued to a small harbour in the fishing village of Folcstan. From there we continued on horseback, following twisting and turning pathways into the hills, dense with undergrowth and fallen gold and brown leaves of oak, chestnut and beech. After an hour we arrived at Lyminge Abbey. Abbess Ethelburga affectionately greeted my niece.

"Erlina! It's so good to see you again! Thank you for coming to us. I know that you will find the Abbey a blessing to you, as you will be to us! Come, let me introduce you to some of our nuns, and show you where you will be sleeping."

The Abbess beckoned to Cadmon and Tola.

"Come, join us; I'm sure you'll want to see everything for yourself, as you've come all this way to bring Erlina to us!"

*

The following morning the Abbess invited me to her study, and we shared news of Coningsburh, our Abbey and the Cathedral.

At last I ventured, "If I may, there's one matter that I wish to raise with you, Abbess."

Ethelburga laughed. "Always just one more thing, Alric! What is it that you wish to ask me? I am of a mind to say yes, so say-on while the mood lasts!"

I leaned forward.

"Mildred," I said, and paused.

Ethelburga's expression changed to one of consternation, but I pressed on.

"Her situation is very different from that of Erlina, quite the opposite in fact. Erlina has longed to be here, while Mildred longs to return to her mother and live at home again in Ratteburg. In brief, Gisela has asked me to petition you for Mildred to return home."

The Abbess sighed, but I pressed on.

"We both know the unfortunate circumstances that brought Mildred here. How long must she be punished for the sins of the father?"

Ethelburga sat silent for a few moments.

"Gisela is a wonderful woman in every respect. She raised me as though I was her own child, and then she married my father after my mother's death, so that Gisela could continue to raise me and give me the very best opportunities in life. Not-one could have been more caring, more loving than she was to me."

Ethelburga stared at the inkwell on her desk, her thoughts far away.

I interrupted her reverie.

"Until you founded the Abbey here in Lyminge, the King gave no thought to Mildred. She had been kept away from Court, living with her mother at Ratteburg, as the annulment of Gisela's marriage to the King required. Then Eadbald saw an opportunity to permanently dispose of his deep embarrassment and confine Mildred here, away from society entirely. She has been here four years now, Abbess, and she earnestly desires to return home."

Ethelburga sat downcast, shaking her head.

"Alric, I deeply regret that what you request is simply not in my power to give. While Eadbald lives, Mildred must remain here in this Abbey. Those are the terms, if she wishes to remain here in the Kingdom of Cantia. If not, Eadbald will have her exiled to Francia!"

*

I was restless, unable to sleep for most of the night. Again and again I churned over Mildred's situation, and the pitifully few options left open to her.

In the morning, to my surprise, the Abbess called me to her study.

"A courier has arrived with a letter from King Eadbald."

Ethelburga paused.

"My brother mentions that he continues to suffer grievously with poor health. He writes that this coming winter is expected to be harsh; and his recovery, if at all, will be slow. He mentions that he has handed over his leadership of the Witan to his younger son, Eorcenbert."

Ethelburga dropped the letter on her desk, her expression deeply troubled.

"Alric, I want to share with you a dream I had last night. Dreams have guided many of our predecessors in the Faith over the centuries—but this dream warned me that Eadbald would not recover from his illness."

The Abbess's weary eyes turned directly on me, noting the shock on my face.

"I must confess that the matter concerning Mildred has given me a sleepless night," Ethelburga continued, her voice trembling.

"My marriage to King Edwin was a very happy one, and we were blessed with the gift of children. My daughter Enfleda deeply misses the Kingdom of the north, where she was born and raised. And one day, perhaps, a king will come who will want to take her for his Queen."

Ethelburga sat twisting the thick white cord she wore about her habit, her eyes welling up with tears.

"Alric, how can I ignore this plea from Gisela, who was my childhood nursemaid and my step-mother? How can I deny my half-sister's plea for Mildred to return home? I cannot," she sobbed. "Mildred must return home to her mother!"

For a while we sat together without a word as Ethelburga sat weeping over Mildred's plight, as a mother would for her own daughter.

Ethelburga wiped away her tears and looked up, her mind and heart resolved as one.

"Alric, I shall give immediate permission for Mildred to return home to Gisela," she said in a brisk tone. "Sometimes we must have the courage to take risks. This is one of them. Take Mildred home with you! I shall tell Mildred personally that she may return to her mother, if that is what she still desires. And I pray that Mildred will find the happiness she so desperately seeks—and so deeply deserves."

*

Cadmon and I stood in the prow, sails unfurling for our return as we reflected on what had come to pass in the last few days. Behind us, seated on the benches, Tola and Mildred sat laughing with relief that at last she was returning home.

The ship cleared the harbour as we set sail for Ratteburg; deep swells from winds the night before threw spray against our prow.

I confided to Cadmon, "I find myself returning in a very different frame of mind than the one I came with."

Cadmon raised an eyebrow. "How so, Alric?"

"Ethelburga gave me some news that might interest you also. King Oswald of Northumbria requested a mission to his Kingdom—from the Isle of Iona, under the auspices of Brother Aidan, an Irish monk. Aidan has chosen the nearby island of Lindisfarne for his Priory—it's close to Oswald's fortress at Bamburgh. His ministry is well received among Oswald's people. Aidan is reaching out to others, and who knows? Soon, he may even arrive at our own shores, Cadmon—and plant and harvest what we have so far refused to do for ourselves."

I paused, reflecting further on where events might lead.

"There's a very different spirit at Ethelburga's Abbey, compared to our own Abbey, and our Cathedral in Cantwaraburh. At Lyminge, they are committed to their new life, demanding as it is, and local farmers and their families flock to the Abbey for support. But back in Cantwaraburh, the scribes that we're training at our Abbey seldom apply their skills to copying the writings of the Fathers and the Prophets. Now we train them to write the King's letters and keep records of the King's farms, the King's laws, the King's shipbuilders, the King's taxes, and not least, the King's trade! Our initial quest has lost its fire; only embers remain. We have lost sight of a priceless goal."

Cadmon put a sympathetic hand on my shoulder.

"You've spoken with great passion, my brother. Do not despair; let us wait and see how matters unfold."

*

It was late afternoon when our ship drew alongside the quay at Ratteburg. I waived to Gisela as she ran down the grassy slope to greet her daughter.

"Alric, you've done it! You've brought my baby home!"

Mother and daughter fell into each other's arms with hugs and tears of joy.

Victorinus was there to greet us, intending to accompany me back to our Abbey, but as it was already late in the day, we accepted Cadmon's invitation to stay overnight at Ratteburg.

Gisela was still concerned that Eadbald might demand Mildred's exile, but Cadmon allayed her fears. "I don't think we'll have much trouble from Eadbald; he is in a poor state of health, and this coming winter will not be kind to him."

Our small party, comprising Cadmon and Tola, Gisela and Mildred, with Victorinus and me, sat down for supper in the candle-lit Mead Hall.

Cadmon asked, "Well, what about the future, Alric? What inspires you now? What can you see?"

I pursed my lips and repeated, "What can I see?"

I had spent so much time complaining to Cadmon about what we couldn't do that his question came as a surprise. All eyes around the table looked expectantly at me. On the roof of the Mead Hall, an owl hooted its eerie night call. I glanced up, and for a moment my mind was a blank as I wondered, did the owl's cry carry a message?

I shrugged the thought aside, and took a deep breath as words long suppressed began to flow.

"My inspiration comes from the words that Queen Bertha once said to me, decades ago. But you know how life is, more and more demands are made, and wonderful inspiration and wisdom dissolve into a dream. So you've asked me, what can I see? I can see religious communities of priests, monks and nuns, not all concentrated together in one small area like Cantwaraburh, but spread out all over this Kingdom—along the coast, on the rivers, in the hinterland. Everywhere. But that is only the beginning. My vision is for many more monasteries of different kinds, ranging from large houses following a Rule of Life—as we did at San Andreas in Rome—to small, loose-knit communities of priests in remote places. Communities, living together in a common life of devotion—in their daily prayers, in giving pastoral care, and providing herbal treatments for all the small communities that cover the land. But more than that; we must set out in pursuit of kingdoms further afield, and not only look to our own. That's what I see."

Cadmon nodded, "Well said, Alric! Without a vision, the people perish. Now, when do you start?"

I laughed, throwing up my hands.

"Sadly, we cannot proceed with anything without the blessing of the Abbot; and we don't have one. So far, we've waited for a successor for nearly two years!"

Cadmon smiled, "Well Alric, from the sound of that owl on the roof, you seem to have one vote on your side already! But seriously, here is something for you to consider. At a meeting a while ago, Prince Eorcenbert called together the Witan in Eadbald's absence. Yes, the Prince is young and inexperienced, I know; but I think his zeal in support of the Church may well be an advantage to you, should he eventually replace Eadbald. Prince Eorcenbert has asked for my support on various matters, and we've met together a few times as Eadbald's health has worsened; so we've made a start. I'll help nudge him in the direction you want to go, but we will have to wait for the next Abbot to be installed. Then you can strike at once, and outline your proposal to the new Abbot. If we can win the support of the King and the Archbishop, the Abbot would hardly refuse to back your plans!"

In the silence that followed, the owl hooted again.

We looked up at the high roof beams to the hole in the rafters, covered by a small protective cover to keep out rain, and allow smoke to escape from the fire.

Victorinus caught my attention.

"Perhaps it's the owl of Minerva, Rome's famous virgin goddess of Wisdom. I think she brings you a message. She's saying, *it's time for bed!*"

XXIV

THE LAST QUEST

February, AD 640

KING EADBALD PASSED away on the twentieth day of January, in the Year of our Lord 640. Eadbald's funeral was lavish by any standards, beginning in the Cathedral and surrounded by crowds of mourners. All of us clergy and monks from Cathedral and Abbey lined up for the procession, both ahead and behind Eadbald's heavy wooden coffin, and we set off to the Abbey for the burial.

I assumed Eadbald would be placed beside Bertha and Ethelbert in their Abbey chapel; but instead, we passed on by, and continued to the Church of St Mary. We glanced at each other, open-mouthed and heads shaking, but said nothing as we entered the Church of San Maria, only a few yards to the east. Here Eadbald was laid to rest—not in the church for worship and prayers, but in a mausoleum, set apart from his parents by his lone burial.

Soon afterwards, with overwhelming support from members of the Witan, Eorcenbert formally succeeded Eadbald as King.

Meanwhile, at the Abbey, we continued to wait for the appointment of a new Abbot and I kept wondering, was it still possible to plant Bertha's vision? Then one night in February, unable to sleep, I found myself sitting on the edge of my straw bed, keeping warm in front of a glowing fire. I took out the gold coin that Queen Bertha had given me at my birth, and her words came drifting back.

"One day, may the Almighty bring him to the place of the great Fisher of Men!"

Mama had recited this to me on every birthday for the first nine years of my life. But why was I remembering it now?

I seemed to hear a chuckle, and in my mind, words began to form. I knew the voice well, and somehow I also felt that this would be the last time.

Queen Bertha spoke.

"Alric, much endeavour still awaits you. The time has now come for you to complete your Quest. Remember the example of the Great Fisherman; follow in his footsteps, and he will be your guide. Now I wish you farewell, until that Eternal Day when we shall meet again!"

Later in the morning a messenger arrived from the Cathedral with a request to meet with Archbishop Honorius at his lodgings close by the Cathedral. I walked briskly down the path to the city wall and through the Queen's Gate to the Archbishop's Lodge, close to the Cathedral's great west door.

"Alric, how good to see you!" Archbishop Honorius began, gesturing for me to sit down. He came straight to the point.

"I know it has been a long time since Abbot Graciosus passed away. How do you find the work of the Abbey now? Is it thriving?"

I outlined as briefly as I could how matters stood at the Abbey, beginning by saying, "It's proceeding well enough, but I also have deep concerns about the future."

Honorius's forehead crinkled in concern.

"What seems to be the problem, Alric?"

I could not waste this rare opportunity, and threw myself into outlining the issues I had discussed with Cadmon a few months earlier.

The Archbishop leaned forward attentively in his chair, his chin resting on his clasped hands, and allowed me the time I needed to express my thoughts.

When I had drawn my thoughts to a close the Archbishop said, "I hear all that you've laid out for me, Alric. I thought you might be thinking in the way you have described. It will certainly take a new

Abbot with vision and stamina to bring about the changes that are needed. But, here—I have a letter for you to read."

I raised my eyebrows in surprise and concern as Honorius picked up a letter from his desk, and passed it to me. I turned the parchment over and looked at the wax seal. I did not seem to have the option to open the letter in the privacy of my room at the Abbey, so I carefully broke the seal, spread out the letter on the desk, and first read the contents carefully to myself, on account of my failing eyesight.

Then, slowly and carefully, I read it again out loud:

"By Royal Assent of King Eorcenbert of the Kingdom of Cantia,

And by divine permission of Pope Severinus, and also

Archbishop Honorius of the Cathedral at Cantwaraburh,

Who, by their good pleasure, bestow upon our best beloved Alric,

Of the Abbey of San Petro e Paulo,

In the Kingdom of Cantia —

The Office of Abbot."

CHARACTERS

Below are the names and brief descriptions of characters in the novel. The names of historical characters are shown in italics.

Aidan, *(d. 609), Irish King of the Scottish/Irish Kingdom of Dalriada. Lost a battle against King Ethelfrith of the Northumbrians 603AD.* (Historical)

Aidan, *Irish monk and bishop. Arr. Lindisfarne in 635AD, d.651. Sent from Iona in Scotland to Northumbria (during the reign of King Oswald) as monk and bishop, performing a very effective ministry during his last sixteen years.* (Historical)

Alric, *(b. 579. A Saxon, oldest son of Galen + Erlina, Sandwic Haven, Kingdom of Cantia; captured and taken in slavery to Rome in December 589AD. Returns to the Saxon Kingdom of Cantia in AD 597. Alric has a second name, Petronius, after a young friend of Alric's dies on the eve of the Pope's launch of his mission to Cantia in AD 596.* (Fictional)

Bertha, Queen, *daughter of King Charibertus I and Queen Ingoberga, given in marriage to Prince Ethelbert in Cantia, 579AD.* (Historical)

Bishop Augustinus, *Roman monk from the Pope's Monastery, San Andreas in Rome; chosen by Pope Gregorius the Great to lead the mission to the Saxon Kingdom of Cantia, 596-7AD.* (Historical)

Bishop Letardus of Senlis *in Francia; in May 579AD accompanied Princess Bertha to Cantia for betrothal to Prince Ethelbert; d .in Cantia, c. 596-7AD.* (Historical)

Bishop Martinus of Turones, *Roman cavalryman, converted to Christ; a towering figure in the religious history of Francia, founder of a monastery, Bishop of Turones; d.397 AD.* (Historical)

Cadmon, younger son of Odelinda and Sighart, Earl of the Ratteburg Estates; Alric's closest friend, also taken in slavery to Rome. (Fictional)

Coifin, *High Priest of the Shrine of Wodin.*

Derian, *Son of Odelinda and Earl Sighart, possessing a mortal hatred of his younger brother, Cadmon.* (Fictional)

Eadbald, *elder son of King Ethelbert and Queen Bertha, successor as King to Ethelbert, c. 616AD; m. Princess Emma of Austrasia, Francia; children: Eorcenbert, Eormenred and Eanswyth; d. 20^h January, 640AD.* (Historical)

Eanswyth, *(between c. 624 - c. 650), daughter of King Eadbald and Queen Emma.* (Historical)

King Eanhere and his brother ***King Eanfrith,*** *joint rulers of the Hwicce people.* (Possibly Historical)

Edwin, King *of Deira and Bernicia (Northumbria, ruled from 616-633; husband to Ethelburga of Kent (Cantia).* (Historical)

Emma of Austrasia, Princess *(c. 595-642, daughter of Chlothar II of Neustria and Haldetrude, married King Eadbald of Kent (c. 618). Children: Eormenred,* **Eorcenbert** *(became King in 641), and Eanswyth.*

Enfleda, *(b.626AD; d.685AD); daughter of Ethelburga + Edwin of Northumbria; (m.* **King Oswiu** *of Northumbria 642AD.* (Historical)

Ethelfrith, *(d.616AD), Saxon King of Bernicia from 593AD;*

(Historical)

Ethelwald: *younger son of King Ethelbert and Queen Bertha.*
   [**NB:** In addition to ***Eadbald,*** it is possible that King Ethelbert had another son, ***Ethelwald.*** The evidence for this is a papal letter to ***Justus,*** (Archbishop of Canterbury from 619 to 625) which refers to a king named ***Aduluald,*** who is apparently different from ***Audubald,*** and refers to ***Eadbald.*** Our ***Legend of the English*** assumes that is the case, in Book 3 of this Trilogy.]

Erlina, *wife of Galen, mother of four offspring: Alric, Tola, Godric and Greta.* (Fictional)

Ethelbert, *King of Cantia, c. 588 – 616 AD; baptised c. AD 597, the key supporter in advancing the mission.* (Historical)

Felix, *Skipper of a merchant-slaver together with crew, Anaxos (navigator), and Souk, (1ˢᵗ mate).* (Fictional)

Franks, *a Germanic tribe that later became the Merovingian dynasty, ruling the kingdoms of Francia.* (Historical)

Galen, *fisherman at Sandwic Haven, husband to Erlina, father of four children, Alric, Tola, Godric and Greta.* (Fictional)

Gisela, *(b. 587) daughter of Count Gundoland, a nobleman from Parisius in the Kingdom of Neustria; nursemaid to Princess Ethelburga, later Queen to King Ethelbert; mother of Mildred. Fictional.*

Godric: *fisherman, and younger son of Galen + Erlina, Sandwic Haven.* (Fictional)

Graciosus, *(d. 638), 4ᵗʰ Abbot of St Augustine's Abbey, Canterbury.* (Historical)

Greta, *youngest child and daughter of Galen + Erlina, Sandwic Haven* (Fictional)

Gundoland, *Count (*Maior domo of Neustria, from 613; Father of Gisela, nursemaid for Princess Ethelburga, Coningsburh, Kingdom of Cantia.)

Haldetrude, *(c. 582-618); first wife of King Chlothar II of Neustria; mother of Emma who married King Eadbald of Kent (c. 618).* (Historical)

Hild, (c. 614–680), Abbess of Whitby. (Historical)

Hussa, *sub-king of Mercia; his Mead Hall on the island of Belspoda, within the Isle of Axenholme.* (Fictional)

John, *(d. 618), 2nd Abbot of St Augustine's Abbey, and a Benedictine Monk.* (Historical)

Jorg, *oldest surviving Saxon warrior of his generation, in the Kingdom of Cantia. Lived his latter years as Earl Sighart's guest at Ratteburg.* Fictional)

Laurentius, *Priest from Rome, formerly an Emissary to Constantinople, later Prior at Pope Gregorius's monastic community at the Lateran Palace in Rome; sent by the Pope to accompany Augustinus to the Kingdom of Cantia.* (Historical)

Mildred, *(b. c 616-18; daughter of Gisela.)* Fictional.

Monks, *living a life of celibacy, prayer and good works; accompany Augustinus to Cantia for the Pope's mission.* (Historical)

Neorth, *Saxon god of fishermen.* (Traditional)

Odelinda, *Wife of Earl Sighart; mother of two sons, Derian and Cadmon.* (Fictional)

Oswiu, *King of Northumbria from 642AD. Oswiu hosted the Synod of Whitby in AD 664, at Whitby Abbey. King Oswiu of Northumbria ruled that his kingdom would calculate Easter by (the Roman dating rather than the Irish and Welsh dating), and observes the monastic tonsure according to the customs of Rome, rather than the customs practised by Irish monks at Iona and its satellite institutions.* (Historical)

Petrus, *monk, accompanied Bishop Augustinus to Cantia; tutor to Alric, later first Abbot of San Petrus & Paulus in the Kingdom of Cantia.* (Historical)
Petronius, *(d. 654), 5th Abbot of St Augustine's Abbey, Canterbury.* (Historical)

Rufinian, *(d. 626) Abbot of St Augustine's Abbey, Canterbury.* (Historical)

Saba, *Earl Sighart's skipper of his trading ship.* (Fictional)
Sighart, *Earl of Ratteburg, including Sandwich Haven and Eastringe; m. Odelinda; 2 offspring, Derian and Cadmon.* (Fictional)
Spelboda, *Queen Ethelburga's Emissary.* (Fictional)

Theodore, *a young monk from San Andreas monastery in Rome.* (Fictional)
Tola, *Saxon,* b. Sandwic Haven, Kingdom of Cantia; m. Cadmon. (Fictional)

Wodin, *chief god of the Saxons* (Traditional)
Wulfrun, *a Frankish priest from Turones in Francia, leader of a contingent sent with the Augustinian mission from Rome to the Kingdom of Cantia.* (Fictional)

PLACES

Adelingesfluet, *Adlingfleet, a village close by the Humbre Estuary and the River Trisentona (River Trent)*

Beltona, *King Hussa's seat, on the Isle of Axholme* (Fictional)

Cantia, *an early name for Kent.*
Coningsburh, *the King's fortress, pronounced 'Kõnings-burra'.* (Fictional)
[NB the C6th-C7th location of King Ethelbert's stronghold remains unidentified. There is no evidence to suggest the fortress was *within* the former Roman city of ***Durovernum Cantiacorum.*** A more likely possibility is on the crown of St Martin's Hill, which may have overlooked the nearby St Martin's Chapel. The area is currently occupied by flats and housing.]

Cantwaraburh, *pronounced 'Cant-wara-burra. A Saxon name that eventually became Canterbury.*
Constantinople, *capital of the Roman Empire*

Dubris, *an ancient harbour in the Kingdom of Cantia; the closest port to Francia. (Historical)*

Eoforwic, *City of York, Northumbria.* (Historical)

Folcstan, (*Folkestone), a small fishing village on the coast, a few miles south of Dubris.* (Historical)

Haethfelth, (Hatfield) *in the Kingdom of Mercia,* a small hamlet hemmed-in towards the north and west by the River Poulter. (Historical)

Isle of Axholme, marshland. (Historical) See note above on King Hussa, and sub-kingdom of Mercia

Kingdom of Cantia, *an early name for the Kingdom of Kent.* (Historical)

Mead Hall, *a Saxon hall for feasting and meeting.*
Monasteries, (Latin Monasterium, Old English mynster) covered a highly diverse group of institutions ranging (by 750 AD) from true Benedictine houses to small, loose-knit communities of priests, and exclusively for both for female nunneries and dual monasteries for both men and women.

Quentovicus, *a trading emporium in Francia, on the Canche River; also the closest port to Dubris.* (Historical)

Raculf, *(Roman Regulbium),* formerly King Eormenric's coastal fort and Royal Hall at the mouth of the Wantsum River overlooking the Temes Estuary.
Ratteburg, (also pronounced *Ratte-burra), a derelict Roman Fort first named as 'Rutupiae', now called Richborough; on a small tidal island on the Wantsum, belonging to Earl Sighart.* (Historical)
Rofesburh, *pronounced 'Rofes-burra;' forerunner of present-day Rochester on the Medway River.* (Historical)
Rome, *(Roma) capital city of Italia, frequently under siege from Langobard warriors and frequently enduring floods, plagues and starvation; formerly centre of the Roman Empire*

Sandwic Haven, *a small fishing village, harbour and trading place in Cantia/Kent.* (Historical)

Scir-wudu: *'bright wood, also known as the Great Forest, and the Sherwood Forest.* (Historical)

Senlis, *(Ancient Roman town of Civitas Silvanectium), 32 miles north-east of Paris; the bishopric of Bishop Letardus; chaplain to Queen Bertha in Cantia.* (Historical)

Stonar, *a small fishing village on the East coast of Cantia; a mile north of Sandwic Haven.* (Historical)

Trisentona, *River Trent.* (Historical)

Turones, *ancient Frankish City of St Martin of Tours.* (Historical)

Wantsum Channel, *the confluence of the Stour and Wantsum rivers and the tidal sea entering from the English Channel and the Thames Estuary.* (Historical)

Waeslinga Straet, a post-Roman, Saxon name for present-day Watling Street. The road begins at Richborough (Ratteburg Fort) and terminates in north Wales. (Historical)

Wathwudu, *Old Norse – wath meaning 'ford', or 'river crossing'; and wudu – Old English, meaning 'wood'.* Present-day West Stockwith. (Historical)

Witenstaple, present-day Whitstable; on the coast, north of Canterbury.

Printed in Great Britain
by Amazon